THE ICE STORM MURDERS

with Homicide in Haliburton

VIRGINIA WINTERS

For my mother, who survived the Ontario ice storm of 1998, alone and isolated by fallen electrical wires, with no power and no heat for three days. She was seventy-seven years old.

Foreword

This volume includes a prequel to The Ice Storm Murders, titled Homicide in Haliburton, a short story that was previously published in A Superior Crime and other stories, as well as on Wattpad.

I note that Canadian English is used throughout.

Introduction

The Ice Storm Murders

In this, the sixth of the Dangerous Journeys series, Anne McPhail and Thomas Beauchamp return to *Inverness*, a back-country lodge, for a wedding. But an ice storm destroys communication and isolates the guests. Then, murder robs host David McKnight of his bride.

The storm rages for days, fuel and power run out and tempers flare.

An attempt on David's life pulls a reluctant Anne McPhail and Thomas Beauchamp into the investigation. Thomas finds another body, and then the killer's attention turns to Anne.

A bonus short story, Homicide in Haliburton, the prequel to The Ice Storm Murders is included.

Who murders multimillionaire Cooper Thwaite in his remote country lodge? Anne and Thomas investigate when a winter storm cuts off any hope of escape.

Homicide in Haliburton

The bright-yellow plane circled lazily upwards into the darkening sky, leaving Thomas and me standing beside our luggage on the shore of the frozen lake. I was glad to be out of the plane and on the ground. The snow was moving in fast.

"I hear snowmobiles, I think," Thomas said.

He had a business meeting at this remote lake on the edge of Haliburton County. We hadn't much chance to spend time together since we met across the border in the small Vermont town of Culver's Mills. Thomas still called it home, although he spent more time in places like New York and Paris and Toronto. I hoped this weekend would help me see where our relationship was going.

The luggage loaded into the trailer behind one of the snowmobiles and helmets lodged on our heads, we began our sedate trip up the hill. A wide veranda wrapped around three sides of the two-story log cabin. Ten bedrooms at least, I thought.

"Have the other guests arrived?" I said to Ted, one of the drivers.

He opened the massive oak front door and waved me through. "Yes, ma'am. You're the last, and just in time too. Weather's coming in."

The first few flakes of the approaching storm swirled through the doorway with us. Inside, the room opened to a vast living area, easily thirty by fifty feet, with walls constructed of massive old logs rising at least ten feet. Brightly-coloured rugs and shabby, over-stuffed furniture warmed up all that exposed wood. Fires burned at each end of the room.

David McKnight, the manager of the lodge, held out his hand in greeting. Long hair that hung free to his shoulders distorted his butler image, though. "Mr. Beauchamp, Dr. McPhail, welcome to Inverness. We've taken your luggage up to your rooms. Would you like to meet everyone, or go ahead upstairs?"

"Let's say hello before we go up," Thomas said.

Of the other guests at the lodge, one of them, Royce Barrington, was a business rival. Their host, Cooper Thwaite, headed an international conglomerate and wanted to involve either Thomas or Barrington or perhaps both, in a new enterprise. Barrington's son and daughter and their spouses had come for the weekend as well but were out cross-country skiing.

Cooper Thwaite was the quintessential Marlboro man: tall, weather-beaten (likely due to time spent on expensive golf courses, I thought unkindly, and it turned out unfairly), chiselled, handsome features and beautifully styled white hair. Only long fleshy ears and a gap between his front teeth marred the overall effect. His attractive wife, Melinda was wife number two or three, judging by her age.

Royce Barrington, on the other hand, wouldn't have been out of place in a small-town Rotary meeting. He was short, a bit heavy, and smiled all over his round face.

Andrea Barrington was and would remain wife number one, I thought. She seemed the sort of content, comfortable woman a man like Barrington would prefer.

"Thomas," Thwaite said, "I am so glad you could bring Dr. McPhail. Welcome to Inverness, my dear," he went on turning to me. He held my hand a few seconds longer than custom demanded, although as I am short, and on the wrong side of forty, I suspected the handholding of being his habit with women.

2

The Barrington children were all in their mid-thirties or so, cheerful and rosy from their adventures in the snow. The males in the room, including Thomas, circled around Melinda Thwaite. Andrea Barrington walked over and sat down beside me on a long sofa. "Have you ever met Melinda and Cooper before, Anne?"

"No, I haven't," I said.

"Do you live in New York?"

"No, I live part of the time in Toronto and also in a country home in Ontario."

I could see her interest fading. I supposed she thought she would never meet me after this weekend.

"Darling Melinda, surrounded by men as usual," she said. Her upper lip curled. "Don't be upset by Thomas, dear; he can't help it. None of them can."

She raised her glass of scotch and drained it. Comfortable Mrs. Barrington had more to drink than was good for her. Her daughter and daughter-in-law, Beth and Karen huddled near the closest fireplace, ignoring their husbands who formed part of the admiring group by Melinda.

Thomas came over to us and suggested we go up to our room and change for dinner.

"What's going on?" I said when we were alone. "Quite a bit of tension down there."

"Tension? I didn't notice. Cooper wanted to talk to me his plans for our discussions this weekend. Who's tense?"

"All the ladies. I do believe they are all a little annoyed with our lovely hostess."

"Melinda? Beautiful as an angel and as thick as she is beautiful."

"Is there always tension when she's around?"

"All the time, honey, all the time," Thomas laughed.

Dinner went quite well—the food was excellent, the wine plentiful, and Mrs. Barrington abstained. I enjoyed talking to her daughter, Beth, a historian who worked for the city of New York, and Beth's husband, Kevin Argyle, a city planner. Her son, Brad, was in business with his father. His wife, Karen, worked for a large charity before her marriage but was "too busy with her social commitments" to continue. Also a few months pregnant she struggled with the no-drinking rule. She sat next to the host, every move scrutinized by her mother-in-law across from her.

Melinda's companions were Brad Barrington and Kevin Argyle. If I were Andrea Barrington, I'd watch my son. He drank heavily and steadily and monopolized Melinda. I wondered if her elderly husband noticed. Karen certainly did.

After dinner, Cooper, Thomas, Royce and Brad moved to the other end of the long room and sat around a low table spread with file folders and laptop computers. Cooper suggested bridge to the rest of us.

I played, but not very well, so left the table to the others, including Melinda who, to my surprise, wanted to play for stakes. I wondered if she was as thick as Thomas joked. After watching for a while, I wandered off to look at the paintings and other objects around the room. Karen disappeared at the first mention of cards.

The evening ended early, for me at least. Thomas' business meeting went on past midnight. When he came to bed, he curled up against me, snuggling his face into my hair. "Sorry about this evening, dear heart. Cooper insisted."

"That's okay. I looked at Cooper's lovely pictures and then came upstairs to read."

Moments later, his breathing smoothed out, and he slept, but I was wide awake again. Knowing from long experience that sleep wouldn't come, I slid out of my side of the bed, put on a robe and started out to find the kitchen.

Wind, not gale force, but strong gusts that swirled snow around the kitchen, piling it into corners, struck me when I forced my way into the kitchen.

Double doors led from the kitchen onto a patio. I could see in the glow from the automatic light in the refrigerator's ice dispenser that something substantial held one of the doors wide open.

Cooper, half-covered with snow, lay in a pool of red, still warm to touch, but dead. Another body. Every time I went on vacation, I stumbled across a corpse.

I pulled myself up from where I had squatted next to Cooper. The cold raced through me, and I shook, a leftover from mild PTSD. What to do now? I wondered where that manager went at night. He would be the logical person to take charge; I didn't want to be the one to tell Melinda.

I pulled open the heavy door, slipped through and let the wind slam it shut again. Better to keep that room as cold as possible for now.

Thomas was snoring when I came in, little flutters of breath that sounded like a tiny car revving up. Too bad to wake him, I thought. "Thomas."

He was instantly awake, one of those people who have no transition between sleep and awareness. "What is it? What's the matter," he said.

He sat up and took my hands.

"I found Cooper's body in the kitchen."

I don't usually blurt out tragic news—bad form for a doctor—but it was the only way.

"Heart?"

"No, a blow to the head. I made sure he was gone and came up to get you. Where is that McKnight fellow?"

"I think he has rooms in the other wing."

Thomas was up and dressed in sweatshirt and pants by the time

I finished giving him all the details of what I'll seen. He thought perhaps I wanted to stay in the room, but there was no way I was spending any time alone anywhere in the house except the bathroom until the cops got there. I was sure Cooper had been murdered.

No bright dawn this morning, just a gradual increase in the light outside. The snow had fallen all night and didn't look to be easing. The wind continued to howl around the eaves, and an occasional loud explosion from the bush marked the death of a tree as a branch gave in to the snow.

David McKnight and Thomas carried Cooper's body to an unheated shed behind the house. Yes, we knew the rule about not moving the body, but we all had to eat, and that kitchen was filling up with snow. McKnight seemed to understand what he was doing because he took picture after picture with his digital camera before he and Thomas carried Cooper's body away.

The rest of us clustered at one end of the living room, drinking coffee while we waited for the kitchen to warm up enough to cook in. McKnight had told us that most of the staff lived out, at a village about ten miles away and were not expected in because of the storm. He would try to organize some breakfast when he had finished contacting the police.

Royce Barrington turned from where he stared out the window at a landscape obscured by blowing snow.

"McKnight didn't say what kind of accident Cooper had. What was it?"

"I'll wait until David and Thomas come back to talk about it."

"Why?"

"Because I think we should all hear it together."

I snuggled further under a warm blanket that Beth Barrington had given me when she found me shivering on the sofa, and tried to ignore the glares from everyone else.

"Come off it, lady," snarled Brad. He and his father loomed over me. It must have looked as menacing as it felt because Thomas shouted at them as he came in with David.

"What the hell do you guys think you're doing? Back off."

"What the fuck happened to Cooper? The doctor here won't tell us. We have a right to know."

Rage twisted Brad's face into an ugly mask.

I turned to Thomas, who sat down beside me and took my hand. "Only Melinda has a "right to know", I said, "and I've already told her, and I'll tell the police. I've been in this situation before."

David interrupted before Brad started again. "I can't reach the police at the moment, folks. The C.B. radio only has a range of five miles, and I can't raise anyone. The phones are down. Our generator will last about 10 hours with the fuel on hand, so I'm going to cut back on the rooms I put the power into—especially this one—and bring in some oil lamps. We'll keep the power for cooking and heating."

He left for the kitchen, lucky guy. I wanted to leave the room too.

"You mean we're stuck in this hole with a murderer!"

Melinda's high-pitched, whining voice came from the stairs.

"Murderer!"

"Who said anything about a murder?"

"I want to get out of here. Kevin, let's get a snowmobile and go." Beth's voice rose above the others as she pulled at her husband's arms.

Melinda glided into the room, fully dressed, entirely made up with every hair in place, looking every inch a merry widow except for the fear in her beautiful eyes.

"Anne and Thomas said he was murdered. One of you killed him."

"You are the one who benefits from his death."

Andrea's comfortable voice had taken on quite a nasty edge.

"You're wrong. I got a settlement when we married, and he put everything else out of my reach. And I loved Cooper, no matter what you might think."

I muttered to Thomas that we were going to need to feed the beasts and left to help David in the kitchen.

While I buttered toast and stirred scrambled eggs, David and Thomas blocked off the end of the kitchen. I supposed they hoped to keep some evidence for the police.

"Have you worked for the Thwaites very long?" I said to David.

"I've worked for Mr. Thwaite for five years. I don't work for her at all, except for when we are up here. Usually, I'm a personal assistant at the office."

Our cooking was interrupted by a sharp rap at the patio door. A tall man in a snowmobile outfit and helmet stood peering in at us. David went over and spoke briefly to him. The man turned and trudged away in the direction of the side door.

"Who was that?" I asked when he came back.

"Guy's name is Mike Lawrence. He got lost in the storm and hunkered down in one of our cabins. When it got to be morning, he realized he was at the lodge and rode up here. I told him to come in through the side door."

"Did you believe him?"

"No reason not to."

"You don't think that he could have killed Cooper?"

"Cooper didn't have problems with Mike."

The food was ready, and we carried it into the living room. Lawrence was just walking in from the hall when we came through the door.

"Folks, this is Mike Lawrence. He stayed in one of our cabins last night, and is joining us for breakfast," McKnight said.

The conversation had turned to business when I went back to the breakfast table.

"Thomas, did you and Cooper agree last night?" Melinda said.

"Does that matter right now?"

"I think so. Cooper told me that if he chose your company,

Barrington would go under. There are a lot of Barringtons here. Maybe one of them thought that I would be more likely to choose their company if he were dead."

"I doubt that anyone here believed you would be running the company if Cooper died," Andrea said.

"No one knew about the prenup, except David, so any one of you could have thought that," Melinda insisted.

"Frankly, dear, no one would have thought Cooper dumb enough to leave you in charge of breakfast, let alone a multi-million dollar company," Andrea said.

"Leave it alone, Andrea," her husband ordered. "I would like to know the answer to that question, though. What would be the effect on your company if he chose mine," he asked Thomas.

Thomas's hand tensed in mine, and the colour rose in his face. "We did come to a tentative agreement after you left us, but it included both of us. I'll show you the outline if you like. It's a waste of time now that he's dead. We'll have to wait for the executor and the board now."

"Wait? I can't wait too long, Tom."

"We'll have to find out how Cooper left the company. Perhaps it's in trust for Melinda."

"No," said Melinda. "He told me that what he gave me when we married is all I would get and even that's all in a trust."

"So you say," Brad Barrington said.

Melinda turned her lovely and not so vacant eyes on Brad.

"If you think that I inherited the company, maybe you killed him. You've always had a thing for me. Maybe you thought you could leave your little wife to her society affairs and marry me, and take the company after he was dead."

"You bitch," screamed Karen, "as if Brad would leave me for a brainless idiot like you. Tell her, Brad, tell her what you think of her."

The Barrington seniors and Beth interrupted, trying to calm the situation. Melinda sat back in her chair, with a Cheshire cat smile on her face as the arguments raged around her.

"Did Cooper have any children?"

The question came out louder than I intended in a lull in the conversation. A deadly little silence ended when Thomas answered no.

"Not any legitimate ones anyway," said Andrea

"What's that supposed to mean," Melinda said.

"He did have a life before you, dear, and he didn't marry all his ladies."

"What would be the position of an illegitimate child," I said.

"Depends on a lot of things, I think," Thomas replied, "especially how the will was written, but I think all children have rights."

When breakfast was over. Thomas and I sat in a remote corner of the room. I thought over the various motives that had surfaced during that ghastly meal. Barrington's financial trouble could have inspired one of them to consider the chances were better with Melinda. Brad, maybe, in spite of what his wife thought. We only had Melinda's word for it that she was cut out of the will. Perhaps she thought her husband was tired of her and ready to move on to wife number four.

And what about other children. There were other people in the house. Who was Kevin Argyle, and what about the pair in the kitchen? One or both of them could have killed him. David said Mike was a stranger, but they were friendly for guys who had just met. Even Beth Barrington was a possibility.

I looked around the room. The Barringtons were huddled together at the breakfast table, but Melinda had disappeared.

For the rest of the morning, I read, and Thomas napped. The Barringtons moved restlessly between their rooms and the living room, all except for Royce who slept soundly on a sofa matching the one Thomas was on. The storm raged on outside. Snowstorms that went on for days were rare in Ontario, but this was day two with no sign of it letting up.

At lunchtime I suggested we all help ourselves in the kitchen. As I finished washing dishes, and how I got elected chief of that chore I didn't know, Karen burst through the door, screaming until Andrea grabbed her and shook her.

"Melinda's dead. I knocked on her door to talk to her, and she's lying on the floor," she gasped when she had regained control.

I dried my hands and towards the stairs. "Why do you think she's dead?"

"She's pale and still and lying on the floor."

"Where's her room?"

"I'll show you," offered David as he followed me out the door and up the stairs.

Melinda and Cooper had separate rooms. Melinda's was surprisingly austere, but perhaps they hadn't spent enough time here for her to bother with décor. A white iron double bedstead stood against one wall. Melinda lay on one corner of the pale-blue bedcover that had been dragged or thrown onto the floor. She was dead and had been for some time. Her skin was cold, and a dark stain of lividity spread along her underarms. The arm had stiffened, so rigor mortis had set in but had no time to leave again. As far as I could remember, that meant it had been several hours since the time of death. Dark purple stains circled her neck. Strangled, I thought, and by a large pair of hands.

David stood in the doorway, keeping the others out of the room. "What killed her? "

"Strangled, I think."

"What in God's name is going on here?

"We're leaving this as we found it," I said as I walked past him out the door and into the crowd in the hall.

"Is she dead?" Thomas said as he put an arm around my shoulders.

"Yes. Let's go downstairs."

The group around the table was past fighting and accusations. Everyone was afraid, or at least all but one. I told them that Melinda was dead but didn't go into any details about what I had found.

"What the hell? That's all you're going to say? She's dead. How did she die?"

Brad Barrington again, angry and blustering.

"Strangled, and I'm saying nothing more until I talk to the police. One of you is a murderer," I said, "and the rest of you shouldn't know what it looked like in there."

"But I do," Karen protested.

"Keep it to yourself," I said.

"What are we going to do?" Beth said.

"Stay together, wait for the storm to stop, call the police," Thomas said.

And we did, moving to the other end of the room, each little group staking out its space and staring uneasily at the others. I like to draw, but I thought that would cause a stir in the current atmosphere, so instead, I looked at each face as though planning a sketch.

Karen's ultra-thin modern face had started to fill out and soften with her pregnancy into her fourth month. She gazed at me, her eyes met mine, but slithered away, perhaps uncomfortable with me looking at her.

The Barrington children both had a strong resemblance to their mother. She must have been attractive when she was younger before alcohol had swollen and distorted her face. I'd thought of it as comfortable, but now she looked boozy and aged to me. Beth and Brad shared her short, upturned nose, round blue eyes and broad jaw.

Kevin Argyle's crooked nose dominated his sharply etched face with its tight skin and angular cheekbones. He was sitting across from David McKnight who looked towards me and away. I had a sudden flash of what?—recognition, I suppose. Those large fleshy ears and that space between the front teeth were those of the dead man. Ears can be a strong genetic trait, even thought as individual as fingerprints. Perhaps it was just a coincidence. Surely, in all the time that they lived together, someone mentioned the resemblance.

Time for me to retreat to the bathroom to think. My mother

always told me to be careful about my face because my thoughts showed. Better to be alone while I decided what to do. I told Thomas where I was going and walked up the stairs. Behind me, David told Mike that he was going to try the radio again.

Karen called to me through the door. "Anne, are you almost finished? I feel sick."

She was a big woman, and the force of her attack drove me back into the room. Her hands reached for my throat as I tried to get my arms up to protect it. I twisted away from her, my elbow hit the bridge of her nose, and she howled in pain and rage. She had her knee on my chest and pulled back her fist. I couldn't breathe, and I couldn't fight her any longer.

"No, you don't." Thomas wrapped his arm around her neck and dragged her off me and out into the hall. Then he was with me, holding me.

"Where is she?" I asked when I could speak again.

"Kevin and Dave have her."

Thomas thought I should lie down, but one stupid mistake was enough. I wasn't going to be alone again until I was back in my little house in Bridgenorth, even if Karen was under lock and key.

The faces of the remaining Barringtons turned toward us, silent and pale.

"Why?" Brad's question. "Why?"

David McKnight answered as he came back into the room. "She had an affair with Cooper last year. That baby she's carrying is his. When he wouldn't leave Melinda to marry her, she killed him. She killed Melinda so that only her baby would be left to inherit the company."

"That's still true," I said.

"No, Cooper left the company to me and dealt specifically with any minor children living at the time of his death. His will gives me the responsibility for looking after their financial needs through a trust he set up in the will."

"How many are there?" I said, fascinated by this Victorian approach to parental responsibility.

"An older boy and a little girl as well as Karen's baby if it lives."

"Why did she attack me?"

"She said you stared at her. She thought you knew what she did"

"Why did he leave the company to you?" Thomas asked.

"I'm his son."

Later that day, the storm cleared, and we contacted the O.P.P. Thomas and I flew out the next day on the little yellow plane. I looked down at the lodge and David McKnight's solitary figure, diminishing as we spiralled up into the bright blue sky.

My feelings for Thomas had grown stronger, but I wasn't sure whether the emotion was love or gratitude for saving my life. A problem to be solved later. He took my hand as the plane levelled off and he sank back into his seat and closed his eyes.

The Ice Storm Murders

Chapter One

The limousine backed out of the driveway of Anne's grey, field-stone house and took the road south towards Peterborough.

"Are we flying fixed wing or in a helicopter this time?" she said.

Thomas's brown eyes met hers. "The company helicopter is meeting us at the airport in Peterborough. It's only ninety kilometres flying so it will take less than an hour to get up there. I'm sorry I rushed you but the weather report for the next two days isn't good."

Poor weather for a wedding, she thought. Perhaps a bad omen for David and his bride.

"I didn't check—"

"High winds and snow."

"It's only November, so maybe it won't last."

The route took them down Highway 28, bypassing most of the city, turning east and then south again to reach the small regional airport.

"Should we talk?" she said.

"Not here."

They needed to some time, she thought, although she wasn't sure what answer she would give him and what would happen to them if she said no. Eleven months since the killer stalked her in

Culver's Mills, six since his mother died and three since the confer-
ence with his children left him with the estate in Vermont and the
burden of caring for it. And now this decision for her. He was
certain of his life, of what he wanted to do, and of what he wanted
from her. Certainty had eluded her through the night before and
into daybreak. Perhaps the wedding this weekend would bring the
question into focus for her.

At the airport, Thomas handed her out of the car and walked
with her to the waiting helicopter. The rotors on the blue and red
aircraft rotated as they clambered aboard. They donned the head-
phones that allowed them to speak to each other and the pilot, but
there was no privacy here either. They rode in the belly of a fabulous
insect, she thought. The land below fell away, and the aircraft
described a lazy arc to the west and north.

The linked waterways of the Trent-Severn canal system chan-
nelled into the waters of the Kawartha Highlands Provincial Park.
They passed over Haliburton Village and a clear blue lake, inexplic-
ably called Head even though it resembled a giant's foot and headed
north towards Algonquin Park and their destination.

Below the Bell helicopter, the lodge and its outbuildings, a red-
roofed cross against the snow, rose to meet them. The pilot off-
loaded them and their luggage and took off.

"He's in a rush," Anne said.

"Weather."

They hurried away from the downdraft towards the house to
meet the couple coming towards them.

Two figures huddled at one end of the expanse of porch around the
lodge.

"What are you doing here?"

"Came for your wedding, darling."

"Came to screw it up for me, you mean."

"Do you want to share all that lovely money or do you want me to mention—"

"How much?"

"Half."

"I'll see you dead first."

"I'll be back."

Could she pull it off, he wondered.

The incoming helicopter drowned out the conversation, and the couple parted, she towards the front door and he to the back.

David and Vanessa waited in the protection of the verandah.

"Who's this, David?" the willowy blonde at his side said.

With her arm tucked into his, David McKnight leaned over and kissed her. How lovely she was, he thought, and how lucky he was. "Anne McPhail and Thomas Beauchamp. He and I do business. She was a doctor and now she travels with Thomas, but I don't think they live together. She's retired but investigates her family history and looked into ours for me. She helped me a lot when Karen killed my dad."

"How?"

"She's observant. Shall we walk out, they've landed."

Ahead of them, the couple rushed away from the aircraft, bent over against the downdraft. Thomas, fiftyish, a lithe 5' 10" or so, towered over his companion, a slight, trim woman in her forties. Her dark red coat set off her face, still wearing a wash of tan. He wondered if she skied with Tom or if they had vacationed somewhere warm and sunny. A little grey in Anne's blonde curls but her face was unlined and cheerful, David noted. Not much changed since her last visit.

When they reached Anne and Thomas, he kissed Anne's cheeks and shook Thomas's hand. "Welcome," he said. "My fiancee, Vanessa Donland."

The formalities over, they strolled back to the expansive log building. Behind them, the helicopter, its jaunty blue and red a bright spot against the darkening sky, flew off to the west.

Inside the lodge, David took them up to their room where someone efficient had already brought in their luggage. Anne remembered that there were back stairs from the kitchen to the upper hallway. Their room opened off the hall on the opposite side to the one they used before. Corner windows opened to the east and north.

"Come down when you're ready," David said.

"We won't be long, and congratulations again, David."

"Thank you for coming," he said. "I have the children with me, and I think you will enjoy meeting them as well."

"Oh, yes."

After David left, Anne and Thomas unpacked and stood in front of the window, its view of the lake overhung with snow-laden clouds. No creatures disturbed the landscape, and the trees were still. Big storm coming, Anne thought. She hadn't checked the weather for the weekend, beyond knowing the forecast was for snow and packing accordingly. There was a ski hill somewhere close that she knew Thomas would want to try. He'd been a world-class skier as a young man, on the European circuit for a while. Or had that been a cover for his more covert activities? She'd never asked him.

She turned back to the room, its log walls disguised with plaster and hung with Inuit paintings. Two club chairs, covered in a print of birds and flowers, flanked a fireplace of grey and pink granite at one end of the room. Tiffany-style lamps stood on simple pine tables beside each. Navaho rugs in the colours of the American southwest —desert pinks and sage—anchored the setting. Thomas added a small log of white birch to the flames that flared and flickered. The familiar smell of burning wood filled the room.

"David's had a haircut," she said. "Do you think Vanessa's influence?"

"I took a meeting with him a month ago. He had short back and sides then but those ears of his showed a bit too much. He's wearing it longer now. Perhaps the responsibility of all those kids motivated the haircut."

"So he would look more conventional to the court? Do any of them live with him full-time?"

"The baby and the little girl. He called the boy Hamish and fought for custody and got it. Proved Barrington wasn't the father. Barrington didn't want the child anyway, David said."

"So he has a ready-made family. Do you know her?"

"Never met her before. Are you okay being here? No flashbacks?"

Flashbacks, she thought. Not yet. The bathroom where a murderous woman trapped her was at the other end of the hall from where they stood. For a moment she was back there, Karen's strong hands at her neck.

She smiled at Thomas and lied. "Not so far."

Thomas stirred the fire with a poker from a set of brass tools that leaned against the fireplace. He spoke to the flames. "Have you an answer for me?"

An answer? Not here, at least not yet. He crossed the room and sat beside her on the bed. Anne reached for his hand and caressed it. The broad fingers of his other hand covered hers and held them still. She shook her head.

He put his arm around her shoulders, and she leaned into him, his tweed jacket rough against her face. "Soon?"

Would it be soon? She hoped so, hoped that she would see her way to him and give him the answer he wanted.

"By the time we leave."

The arm around her shoulders tightened and released her. "We should go down. David said cocktails."

They changed into jeans and colourful sweaters, the usual lodge wear, and joined the others in the great room.

At the foot of the stairs, the room opened to a living area, easily thirty by fifty feet, with log walls rising at least ten feet. Brightly-coloured Navaho rugs and overstuffed furniture upholstered in a faded print warmed up all the exposed wood. Fires, releasing the scent of pine and apple, crackled at either side of the room. Along one wall, bottles in vibrant blues and reds and cut-crystal glasses reflected in a horizontal mirror. An impersonal room in spite of the comfort, Anne thought. Nothing changed from when Cooper Thwaite or his decorator chose the rugs and the fabric. Nothing here that reflected David or his taste in art or furnishings or colour.

A white-coated waiter circulated with trays of shrimp and one-bite pastries, but a television set beside the further fireplace absorbed the attention of the assembled guests. Brad Barrington, a lanky forty-year-old with prematurely-greying hair and acne-scarred skin, his square jaw reflecting his mother's, settled into an armchair and kept his eyes on the television. He ignored his mother, Andrea, who perched on a nearby sofa. His eyes focussed on Vanessa when they slanted away from the television. He was a heavy, steady drinker, Anne recalled.

Another couple, Beth and Kevin Argyle, sat together on a loveseat with a clear view of the screen. Beth, too, shared her mother Andrea's square jaw, round blue eyes, and upturned nose. A historian for the City of New York, she had no children, whether by design or not, Anne didn't know. Her husband worked as a city planner. His crooked nose dominated his sharply-etched face with its tight skin and angular cheekbones.

The long-legged woman reading the weather gestured to a weather pattern that encompassed all of eastern Ontario. Her sing-song voice barely concealed excitement at the coming storm.

How odd of David, Anne thought, to replicate the house party of the weekend his father died. Except for Karen, of course. She shivered.

"Cold?"

"Goose on my grave," she said, the answer from her childhood.

David waved them over. "I think you all know Anne McPhail and Thomas Beauchamp."

Terse murmurs acknowledged the introduction, but everyone's attention swivelled back to the screen.

"Ice storm warning," David said.

"When?" asked Anne.

"Tonight and tomorrow. I'm sending the staff home now."

He left them, spoke to the waiter, and hurried with him to the kitchen.

Anne had lived through two major ice storms and the havoc they brought—downed power lines, no communication, and people cut off for days with little food or fuel. Perhaps it was all weather-expert hyperbole.

Vanessa, dressed now in white silk trousers and shirt separated by a gold belt, stared after him, her brow wrinkled in confusion. The informal dress code at the lodge had changed, Anne thought. Nothing to do about it now, she decided, remembering that she brought only one formal outfit, for the wedding, and the rest casual tops for her favourite jeans.

"Will that change your plans?" she said to Vanessa.

Vanessa shot a venomous glance and said, "Certainly not."

What was that about, Anne thought. She wasn't responsible for the storm.

"It might, darling, if the minister can't get here," said David, coming up behind her and putting his arm around her.

Vanessa gasped, but before she spoke, the doorbell rang.

"I thought everyone was here who was coming this evening. Did you invite someone without consulting me?" Vanessa said.

"That must be Trevor and Carmel," said a voice behind them.

Andrea, who looked like a pleasant grandmother with her round face and bright blue eyes, had a severe drinking problem and bad temper, Anne knew. She glanced at Thomas, who raised an eyebrow and shrugged.

"I thought you wouldn't mind, David, since others of my family is here," said Andrea.

Her voice dragged. Drinking still a problem for her then, Anne thought. What a jolly weekend this would be.

The roar of the staff vehicles racing away from the lodge drowned out the conversation at the door between Andrea and the arriving couple. Cold seeped around the corner from the foyer and into the long room.

"Everyone, please meet Trevor and Carmel Baker," Andrea said.

"How are these people your family, and why did you ask them?" said Vanessa, her voice icy.

Trevor, a stocky man with flaming red hair and a shy manner, rocked back on his heels. His wife, her oval madonna face framed with thin chestnut curls, squeezed his arm.

"Trevor is Karen's brother and Hamish's uncle," said Andrea.

Karen's brother. How difficult was that going to be, Anne thought. She glanced at Thomas, but his eyes were on the scene outside.

"If we're unwelcome, we can leave," Trevor said.

As if in answer, the storm hit, an onslaught of wind that howled in the chimneys and rain that pelted the windows.

"Not for a while," said Thomas.

Chapter Two

A few moments later, a young woman, twenty-five years old or so, came down the stairs and crossed the room to where they stood. She carried a toddler in her left arm and held hands with a child perhaps five years old, her blond curls subdued into ponytails on either side of a gamine face. Her face broke into a delighted grin, she detached herself from her minder, and launched herself at David, hugging his legs. He scooped her into his arms.

"Uncle David, Eloise didn't want to come, but I fussed at her, and she brought us."

"You know you're not to fuss at Eloise."

"But the rain is so loud."

"It's all right. Everyone, this is my ward, Olivia, her nanny Eloise Leclerc and baby Hamish."

He put Olivia down and took the toddler into his arms.

"Dadda."

Ready-made family indeed, Anne thought. Why does the little girl call him Uncle? Perhaps he shares custody with her mother. She glanced at Vanessa and was startled by the lip-curling disgust on her face.

"David, our guests need some dinner," Vanessa said.

"Eloise, take the children into the kitchen,"

"But I want to stay," Olivia said.

"Go with Eloise," Vanessa said.

Eloise, a dark-haired, dark-eyed woman with a square face and a resolute jaw, took the baby from David's arms, grasped Olivia's hand, and marched to the kitchen door.

The little girl's eyes filled with tears and gazed back at David before going through the door.

Anger flashed across David's face, turning him at that moment into an image of his dead father. "Was it necessary to send them out?" he said.

"Yes. Food is laid on next door," Vanessa said and sailed away towards the dining room.

Waiting for the others to go ahead, Anne said to Thomas, "Not so jolly with children, is she?"

"You caught that look?"

"I did."

"Let's go in. This may be our last hot meal. The way the storm is building up, we may lose power."

Windows soared on two sides of the dining room, the equal in width to the living room but shorter by twenty feet, a pleasing square. A stone fireplace on the end wall lit the scene with orange flames while overhead two art-nouveau chandeliers cast a leafy pattern across white linen. Three ruby-shaded lamps glowed down the centre of the table. Pleasing smells of roast beef wafted down the room. Platters filled the centre of the table and old-fashioned silver chafing dishes lined up along the sideboard.

Anne and Thomas found themselves at opposite sides and opposite ends of the table. Anne's companion on her right was David at the head of the table; opposite sat Andrea Barrington. Kevin and Beth took chairs on either side of the table. Both dressed in fashionable New-York black. It didn't suit Beth. She should wear vivid colours to accent her dark hair and deep blue eyes. Kevin, looking robust and healthy even with his gaunt face, smiled from time to time at his wife. Perfect American teeth, Anne thought before recalling that they were, in fact, Canadian even though they lived in New York.

A small group for a wedding. She assumed other expected guests missed the dinner because of the storm. Vanessa glowered at the other end of the table with Thomas on her right and Brad at her left.

"To my beautiful bride," said David, raising his glass.

"To Vanessa," echoed around the table as they all lifted champagne flutes.

An excellent wine, Anne thought, but across the table, Andrea placed an untouched glass back on the table. Why did Andrea mime drinking the toast? She usually didn't miss a chance to drink champagne. At her right, David's eyes focussed on Vanessa at the other end. A fleeting thought or something furrowed his forehead, he lowered his head, and frowned at the tablecloth.

The table chatter went on, drowned out at intervals by a fresh onslaught of ice against the windows from the black void beyond. At times, thunder boomed, and lightning lit the scene. Ice coating the needles of the fir trees that surrounded the lodge flashed with each strike.

"Thundersnow," Brad said.

"Hardly snow," Vanessa said. "Let's return to the living room."

Anne wondered who would clean up the table, but decided she wasn't offering this time. The last visit to the lodge, she spent most of her time in the kitchen preparing meals and washing dishes.

Two dogs, one a black standard poodle with a puppy clip and the other, grey and shaggy and of mixed ancestry hurried off the sofa where they'd curled up near the fire.

"David, get your dogs out of here. Now their dirt and hair will be all over the sofa," Vanessa said.

"Come," David called to the dogs from the kitchen door.

The shaggy dog, Max, bounded over to him, but Andy, the

poodle, stopped to say hello to Anne, who rubbed the dog's chin and scratched behind her ears.

"Put them outside," Vanessa said.

"The ice-storm," David said.

"What does that matter? They have a kennel."

"No. Not tonight."

Vanessa followed him into the kitchen, and raised voices reached them for a moment before she returned. Brad turned the television on again to the weather channel.

Returning, Vanessa, flushed and brusque said, "Must we watch that? Liqueurs or cognac, anybody?"

"Yes, cognac," said Andrea.

"We're leaving tonight if the weather is going to let up," said Brad.

"Before the wedding?" Vanessa said.

"I doubt that you're getting married this weekend," said Andrea, in a satisfied voice.

"David, David," Vanessa screamed.

After he came through the door, she rushed to him and whispered. He put his arms around her, but she tossed them off and raced up the stairs. David ran up after her.

Beth cocked her head at Kevin, suggesting they follow. They left Anne and Thomas sitting alone in the darkening room.

"Let's go to bed," Thomas said. "All this drama is way too much."

They reached the foot of the stairs when a doorbell rang an SOS and fists pounded at the kitchen door. They raced in as David clumped down the back stairs.

Ice on the snowmobile helmet obscured the features of the man at the door. Ice coated his parka and, already thawing, dripped onto the grey-tiled kitchen floor.

When the man lifted off the helmet, Anne recognized Mike Lawrence, a fellow who arrived during their last stay in

Haliburton in time to help with the guests. A good-natured local man with an engaging grin and thinning dark hair, he'd been Anne's partner in dishwashing and food preparation. He was affable and unflappable. Anne liked him and appreciated his common sense.

"What brings you out in the storm, Mike?" David said.

"I was out, checking my traps before the ice hit. I just made it. Machine died out there."

"You'd better take off that wet parka and pants," said Anne.

"Hi, Anne. You and Thomas here for the wedding? Say, David. What about the reverend? Is he here or—"

"Nope."

"So no wedding tomorrow?"

David shook his head and grimaced. "Not unless it thaws overnight and Vanessa is none too happy. I'm glad you're here. I'm going to need help keeping that furnace going."

Mike nodded his head and pointed a hand towards the wood box by the stove.

"You got plenty of wood?"

"Yeah, if we can get to it."

"I thought you had a heat pump, David?" Anne said.

"It failed in October and I put in one of those outdoor boilers until the spring. But with this ice, I don't know."

"She'll be okay if we can keep her fired up," said Mike. "Is she okay for now? I'm about froze through."

"Yes, for a while."

At that moment, the lights flickered and failed.

"How long before the generator kicks in?" Mike said.

"Two minutes."

"How much fuel do you have?"

"Twenty-four hours, give or take."

"Think it will be enough?"

"If we're careful."

Somewhere upstairs, someone, Vanessa, Anne thought, shrieked for David. He cocked his head but waved the summons away.

Anne and Thomas left them as they discussed plans for conserving fuel and climbed the stairs to their room.

Their bedroom repeated the theme from the living room below, with exposed logs and flooring of reclaimed pine. Old as the wood was, the walls still gave off the woodsy scent of cedar. More personality in this room, she thought, more comfortable than the communal spaces.

David told her his father commissioned a craftsman to make the bed from timber rescued from the depths of the Ottawa River. The ancient pine glowed in the light from the stained glass shades of lamps standing on bedside-tables of the same wood. Across from the bed, French doors opened to a balcony. Flames leaped and crackled in the fireplace. Thomas fed it, undressed, and climbed into bed.

"How lovely," Anne said.

"Not as lovely as you are."

She undressed, taking care to hang her clothes neatly in the closet. If they stayed for more than two days, she would run out of clothes.

Later, with her head tucked into Thomas's bare shoulder, she said, "Odd all the same people from last year are here."

"I doubt David intended to have only this bunch. I think the rest of the guests cancelled."

"Somehow, I wish we had too."

Chapter Three

Early the next morning, Eloise opened the door to the back stairs. Voices in the kitchen reached her, and she crept down to where she could see into the room. That was Mike, she thought. And Vanessa.

"Hello, sweetheart. How's it going?"

"Don't call me that. What are you doing here? I thought we agreed—"

"I got caught in the storm on my way back to town."

"Leave."

Vanessa, dressed in a filmy lace peignoir, her face suffused with an unbecoming red, pushed Mike towards his coat. He grabbed her wrist and turned her to face the window over the sink. "No chance. Have you checked outside?"

"I don't care."

On cue, an elderly pine across the field shrieked as the leader branch fell under the weight of the ice. Ice-thickened rain coated the windows and obscured the view of the broken giant.

"You're not getting married today, anyway."

Mike poured two cups of coffee and sat at the cafe table in the windowed alcove. Vanessa hesitated but slipped into the chair opposite. "We could pretend you're one of those mail-order ministers?"

"No, we couldn't. Not in Ontario. You need a license from the province and a proper marriage license for the happy couple. Don't you remember from the first time?"

"I'd rather not."

The dogs, roused by the voices, trotted into the kitchen and sat by Mike, noses up and eyes begging.

"Get rid of those."

"What do you have against the dogs?"

"Dogs, kids. They're all going after we're married and that woman will be out of here, too."

"What woman?"

"Eloise."

"The cute little Frenchie? Why?"

"She's in love with David."

"And she's younger."

Eloise, her heart pounding, tiptoed up the stairs to the nursery. Get rid of her and the children, not to mention the dogs. What was she going to do? Should she tell David?"

Vanessa swivelled in her chair towards the staircase. "What was that?"

"What was what?"

"I heard something on the stairs. Where did you put the dogs?"

"The living room. Where else? What's the matter with you? I thought you were getting all you wanted from this act of yours."

"He owes me."

"Who owes you?"

"David, his father. All the Thwaites."

Mike passed his hand over the grey-streaked stubble on his chin. Why was he looking at her like that? What did he know that she didn't?

"You'll be in big trouble if anyone finds out."

He wanted money. That was what he said before.

"I don't have any money."

"You will, Van. You will. David is a very generous guy."

"You'll not—"

"Gravy train for both of us, my sweet."

"I want my share. The old man was my father, too."

"Take that up with David. Did the old man know you existed?"

"Tell David. Are you crazy? No."

He knew everything, she thought. What was she going to do?

"Relax. I'm not here to sink your boat. You'd better dress. I hear people out there."

"That McPhail woman was watching me."

"She watches everything. Hurry."

She rushed up the back stairs to her room, locked the door behind her, and flung herself on her bed. What could she do? Could she trust Mike?

That same morning, Anne propped herself on an elbow and gazed out at the leaden sky. Freezing rain pelted down, so heavy and thick with ice that it obscured the lake and the forest. Thomas mumbled, turned over, and slept on. She dressed and left for the kitchen.

"Good morning, Eloise," said Anne, cutting bread at the counter as the young woman trooped in with the two children, Olivia in a fluffy pink housecoat decorated with butterflies and Hamish in a miniature dressing gown in the dark blue and red McKnight tartan over his Curious George pyjamas.

Anne popped slices of bread into the toaster and set the percolator on the woodstove. Coffee was always a welcoming smell, she thought, as the bubbling began.

"Is it? I can't see past all that ice."

"We're safe inside, warm and dry and food coming. Might be worse."

* * *

The kitchen, its log walls covered with drywall painted a cheerful daffodil, overlooked the field behind the house, or did when the view wasn't obscured by ice. A pine table surrounded by eight press-back chairs filled the middle of the room. Anne found scarlet mats in a drawer for each place setting and handed service-able white plates to Eloise, along with the children's eggcups, a puppy for Olivia and a rooster for Hamish.

"I'm sorry, Anne. I heard—"

Eloise's dark eyes misted with tears, but before she spoke, David and Mike, coming in, tramped snow and ice off their boots and hung their parkas near the woodstove.

"Who got this going?" said Mike.

"I did," Anne said."We had one in our cottage when I was young."

"Can you cook on it, too?" asked David.

He lifted the old white percolator from the hotplate on the stove, smelled and poured himself a cup.

"If needs be."

"And how are you this morning, Olivia?" said David.

"I didn't sleep a wink."

Anne and Eloise swallowed their laughter as David sat down beside the serious little girl. "And why not?"

"Something scratched at my window."

David put his arm around her. "It's only the storm, the same as when the rain and the wind rattle the windows. This time the rain turned to ice instead of snow."

"I don't like it."

"It will stop soon. Here is Eloise with your egg and toast soldiers."

Eloise moved to the stove to get another egg for Hamish.

So that was how it was, thought Anne, as she intercepted the smile and adoring glance that Eloise flashed towards David. But David didn't seem to notice as he dipped rectangles of buttered toast into the soft-boiled egg for each child in turn.

"How is the wood supply holding up?" Anne asked.

"Plenty for now," Mike said.

"Would you bring more for the stove when you go out next?"

"Are you planning to do the cooking again this time?" Mike asked.

"When did you do the cooking here?" Eloise asked.

No one answered for a moment, and David kept his eyes on the children.

"We were in a similar situation in a heavy snowstorm a year ago. Everyone had to pitch in."

"The children are finished," David said. "I'll take them into the living room. You and Anne eat your breakfasts."

When they were alone, Eloise turned to Anne.

"What has gone on here? There seems to be some secret."

"Has no one told you about Hamish's mother?"

"No."

"She became deranged early on in her pregnancy and killed David's father and his fiancee. She's in prison now. She was married to Brad Barrington."

"Murders? Here?"

Eloise's face paled. Anne sugared her drink and handed it to her.

"I think you should understand who these people are."

"If Brad is Hamish's father, why does he not live with him?"

"Because Cooper Thwaite was his father and David's father."

"And Olivia?"

"Also Cooper's. I don't know who her mother is."

"So tangled. But I thought perhaps they were David's children, he loves them so."

"Yes, he does. He's their brother."

Raised voices from the other room brought them to the door of the kitchen.

The children sat on the floor of the living room, playing with giant lego and minute lego people. Above them, a tide of angry voices crashed and ebbed.

"What makes you think I want messy children all over the living room floor when our guests arrive?"

"Vanessa—"

"Don't Vanessa me. Look at them. Egg all over their faces and jam on their hands. I want them upstairs where they belong."

Olivia inspected her hands and Hamish's face. "We don't have egg and jam—"

"Don't contradict me, Olivia. Where is that little witch who is supposed to be looking after them? Was she too busy mooning after you to wipe their grubby hands."

"What are you talking about—mooning."

"Don't play games with me, David. The guests will be arriving and—"

Olivia pulled Hamish after her and ran up the stairs. Eloise left Anne's side and stepped back into the kitchen.

"No," said David.

"What do you mean, no?"

"Have you looked outside or further than your nose. No one is coming. Not the guests, not the minister, not the musicians. Not today."

Vanessa shrieked and disappeared into the dining room. David hesitated but returned to the kitchen. The door swung closed behind him, and he slumped into a kitchen chair.

The rain laid siege to the windows, covering them with a frozen curtain. The dogs nuzzled him, one to a side. Max, worried, rested his shaggy head on David's knee and watched his face from below his bushy eyebrows. David ran his hand behind the dog's ears and scratched.

"So that's it. No wedding. No family."

"I wouldn't say that, David. You still have the children and Eloise to help you," said Anne.

Eloise said, "I have to go to the children."

She ran up the back stairs.

"What did she mean Eloise mooned after me?"

"You must pay better attention after this."

David pushed back through the door into the living room just before Thomas clattered down the stairs to the kitchen.

Upstairs, Olivia listened at the nursery door. When no one followed them up the stairs, she scampered down the hall to Vanessa's room. Inside, she lifted the lid on the beautiful box on the table with the mirror behind it. Once before she had opened the box but Vanessa caught her, and said she would spank her if she found her there again. Olivia didn't know what spank meant, but it sounded bad. But there were necklaces and rings in the box, all glittering and beautiful.

She explored the box, trying on a sparkling ring with bright red stones and plain glass ones. At least they looked like glass to her. They were pretty but not like the red and green and blue ones. She pulled up the top tray. Papers, just papers. Why would Vanessa keep papers in the box with her jewellery? If only she could read.

Someone was coming. Footsteps stopped outside the door but went on. Now she was scared. What if Vanessa found her? The spanking thing sounded scary. She couldn't put the tray back in over the papers. She stuffed one of them into her pocket and tried again. She slammed the top and raced from the room back to the playroom.

"Olivia, where have you been?"

"I went to the bathroom."

"Were you in Vanessa's room again?"

"No."

Olivia was scared again. She told Eloise a lie. What if they sent her away? Vanessa wanted to send her away. What if Eloise wanted to send her away too? When she peered up at Eloise, she saw tears on her face. "I'm sorry. Don't cry."

Eloise sat down on the playroom rug beside Olivia and hugged her. "Not your fault, ma chère."

A knock at the playroom door brought Eloise to her feet, wiping her face with her hands. Brad and Andrea came in. "We'll play with the children while you have breakfast, Eloise."

Olivia's face drooped. Why did they have to come?

"Thank you," said Eloise and left.

"What would my darling boy like to play?" said Andrea, picking the toddler up and covering his face with kisses.

"He wants to play Lego," said Olivia.

"Don't talk for Hamish," said Brad.

Olivia wandered over to the play table and reached for her crayons. Behind her, the grown-ups talked to Hamish and to each other.

"He's such a lovely boy, isn't he, Brad?"

"Yes, Mom. Enjoy him while you can."

Andrea clutched Hamish to her, and he squealed. Why was she holding him so hard, Olivia thought. He didn't like it.

"There, there, Hamish. Grandma's sorry."

"What do you mean?"

"After they're married, he'll cut off your access, and you won't see Hamish again."

"Vanessa doesn't like them."

"Vanessa likes David's money."

What was access? What were they going to cut? Olivia put her head down on the desk and cried.

"Now you've upset Olivia. You'd better go," Andrea said.

Olivia kept on crying. Maybe she would leave too.

Chapter Four

Thomas passed Eloise on the stairs.

"What's going on here?" said Thomas when he came into the kitchen. "Eloise looked as though she was about to cry."

"Sit down, and I'll tell you."

Before she described the scene, Thomas walked to the doors, made sure no one was listening and sat again.

Cautious, Anne thought. He'd slipped into what she called, to herself, his spy mode. Calm, pragmatic, unemotional.

"What happened afterward?"

"David came in here and talked about how much he wanted a family and how much he loved the children. He thinks it's over with Vanessa."

"After one fight?"

"Fundamental issue, though."

He reached for her hand and rubbed it between both of his. Her hand must be cold, she thought.

"What about us? Is the problem between us fundamental too?"

"The problem with me is fundamental. I—"

Vanessa swung open the kitchen door from the dining room, took one look and yelled for David.

"What is it this time?" he said when he came through the door from the living room.

"These damn dogs are in the kitchen. Put the filthy beasts outside."

"Come," David called to the dogs from the kitchen door.

The poodle danced over to David, who rubbed her neck and whispered to her. Max shook his shaggy head and ambled towards the door to the living room.

"I said put them outside."

"My house, my dogs, my rules," said David.

He opened the door, and the dogs ran through into the living room.

Vanessa followed.

"No privacy in this kitchen," Thomas said. "We'd better follow and make sure no one is injured."

The others—the Barringtons, Mike, and the Bakers, but not the Argyles—huddled at one end of the long room far from Vanessa who railed at David and then struck a pose with one arm on the mantle of the fireplace. The mantle was a shade too tall for her, Anne thought, making her ever so slightly awkward. Not perfect.

She was lovely, though, even with her ears exposed. Vanessa wore her blond hair pulled back in a sleek chignon, diamonds flashing from the lobes of her long ears that stood a little too far away from her head. If they were to have children of their own, ears would be a problem. It was odd, she thought, that Vanessa and David's were so similar. But perhaps, with the way things were going, it wouldn't be an issue.

The dogs bounded over to Trevor, who rubbed an ear on each and received kisses on his nose when he put his face close to theirs.

"Ugh. How can you, Trevor?" said Vanessa.

"I like dogs and dogs like me," he said.

Beth and Kevin came in and again sat a little apart from the group. Anne caught a frown on Andrea's face, directed towards Beth, Anne thought. What was that about?

The phone rang.

For a moment, no one moved. David picked up the phone, scowled and said, "Brad, the call's for you. The prison."

"Why—"

"No idea."

Brad walked the phone into the dining room. The guests milled about, straining to hear his conversation while pretending to chat about the weather.

Vanessa and David whispered in a corner. The scarlet of her face, still present from her anger, deepened.

Anne overheard part of the conversation.

"I will not, and if that's how you feel, we're done," David said.

Vanessa stalked to the window and pretended to look out at the storm.

A moment later, a white-faced Brad stumbled back into the room and collapsed in a chair beside his mother.

"What is it?"

"Karen's dead."

"How?" someone asked.

"Opioids."

Someone gasped, but when Anne looked around, she saw only concern on the faces of the others. Brad sobbed into his mother's shoulder. Her eyes glistened, and she patted his back. On her other side, Trevor hid his face in his hands. His shoulders heaved. Carmel stood beside him, her emaciated hand stroking his hair. Beth walked over to her brother and sat on his other side and put one hand on his arm. He shrugged her off, but she stayed beside him.

Andrea glared at Anne.

"You, it's all your fault."

"What—"

"You sent her there. You had to poke around, stirring things up. She would be at home with Hamish except for you."

She lunged across the room towards Anne, stumbled, and fell, but David saved her from hitting the floor. She flailed at his chest.

"Get away from me."

"Andrea." David said.

"You're the same. Why did you have your stupid party?"

Andrea screamed and ranted until Brad and Beth dragged her up to her room. Kevin hunkered down in a club chair, his face impassive.

Anne collapsed into a chair, hugging her arms to her chest. Thomas stood beside her, his hand resting on her shoulder. "A drink?" Thomas said. "Cognac?"

"A little."

What a nightmare, Anne thought. Trapped with a madwoman, a grieving family, and battling bride and groom.

"I thought she was a murderer. Why all the hysteria?" Vanessa said, not too quietly, to David.

"She was his wife before she was a murderer."

"That doesn't explain the mother-in-law or was that just alcohol? Don't look at me as if I'm the crazy one. You're all nuts."

She twisted away from David and ran up the stairs.

The others drifted away, leaving only David, Thomas and Anne in the darkening room. The storm, as though empowered by the rage in the house, shook the windows and pelted them with ice.

"I'm sorry he has to stay here," David said.

"I'm sure all of them would prefer to be elsewhere," said Thomas.

"He said an overdose of opioid but he didn't say if it was suicide or accident or murder."

"Or how she wasn't found it time," said Anne.

"In time?" David said.

"For Narcan, the antidote."

"Do you still carry Narcan with you?" Thomas asked.

"Always. With this opioid crisis you never know when you might be the only one who can help. I wondered how, in a facility where the prisoners are supposed to be watched, this happened."

"Went to sleep and didn't wake up, I imagine."

Eloise came down the stairs and called to David. "Would you say goodnight to the children? The storm is making them anxious."

"In a moment."

"You have a lovely family," Anne said.

"All I ever wanted was a family and now I almost have one. I'd better go to them."

"I't's a shame she doesn't share his desire," Anne said after David walked up the stairs.

"Should we talk about us, dear heart."

He enveloped her in his arms.

"We know about us. I have to decide about what I should do and my thoughts aren't clear."

"When you're ready—"

"Let's go up."

Eloise sat on an armchair near the play table. Olivia worked on drawing with her favourite purple crayon and Hamish built towers with his over-sized Lego. David came in after knocking on the frame of the open door. Hamish ran to him and put up his arms. David scooped him up.

"Dada."

"Hi, little guy. What are you building?"

"Big."

Hamish followed his word with a string of babble. David put him down, Olivia took his hand, and pulled him to the table to see her latest creation. "Uncle David, I'm drawing our house."

"Let's see."

"I see you drew the living room and all the people."

"Yes. Then I'll draw some more rooms."

Eloise searched David's face. So much love, she thought. Why did he bring that awful woman into their lives? What if she asked if she was staying after the wedding? She needed to know. "David, could I ask you a question?"

"Of course. Something wrong?"

"Perhaps. I wondered if I would have a job after you were married. Perhaps Vanessa would like to choose her own nanny for the children."

David's eyebrows shot up. "They aren't Vanessa's children."

"But—"

His face reddened and his mouth became a thin line and a deep furrow appeared between his eyes. Was he angry with her?

"You work for me. Vanessa has no say and will have no say in my staffing decisions, especially as regards the children."

"That might be uncomfortable. I heard her tell that man, Mike, that she wanted all of us to go—me, the dogs, the children."

"You misunderstood."

"No, I didn't but I'm sure she will deny it. That is why it will not be comfortable for me here."

She moved away from him and gazed out across the field. The ice didn't coat the nursery windows but across the field, birch trees bowed to the ground under their burden and behind them stood two venerable pines, their tops scarred where the weight had severed the main trunk. Wind shook icicles from the trees and smashed them on the frozen snow below.

"Please don't do anything rash. This weekend is strange for all of us and now with the tragedy—"

"What tragedy?"

"Brad's ex-wife, Trevor's sister died in prison. They telephoned this morning."

"Hamish's maman?"

"Yes."

"Il pauvre garçon."

"Will you stay after the storm?"

"For a short time."

"Thank you."

For a moment Eloise thought he was going to hug her but he stepped back, said goodbye to the children, and left.

How could she leave him? What would she do without him and without the children? That woman was so horrible.

"Don't cry, Eloise. Uncle David won't let anything bad happen."

Olivia's little hand patted her back.

"I hope not, chèrie. I hope not."

Chapter Five

Trevor and Carmel followed Brad, his sister, and Andrea upstairs but Brad slammed shut the door to Andrea's room, and they continued down the hall. Light filled their small room, tucked away around a corner of the hallway, despite the ice that coated the windowpanes. One door led to a bathroom, another to a closet. Carmel said she liked the room; liked the ice-blue colour that predominated. Too cold for him.

Carmel drooped in one chair while Trevor sat in the other, one long-fingered hand covering his eyes.

"Perhaps she would rather die than spend twenty-five years in prison?"

"Don't say that. The lawyers appealed the length of the sentence. Someone killed her."

"Did Brad say she was murdered?"

"No. But Karen didn't do drugs."

"Perhaps she started."

Carmel's voice trailed off to a whisper. What was he going to do? She got worse every day. Even in the few hours since they arrived, she seemed to dwindle.

"David and Vanessa aren't getting along," he said.

"I hadn't noticed."

"The wedding might be off."

She raised a languid hand and let it fall into her lap where it lay, white and still. So pale. The doctor said her iron was low and gave her pills, but she wouldn't take them.

"What does it matter?" she said.

"If he's not married, David will find it difficult to convince the court he should keep Hamish from his family, from us."

"From us?"

A frown appeared between her eyes and she cocked her head at him. "From us?"

"I think we should petition the court. I'm his family, too."

"They won't give him to us because of me."

Silent tears dribbled over her cheeks and dropped, unheeded on her silk shirt.

"If you thought we could adopt Hamish, you would get better, eat again."

"They'll likely make up. People do."

"Maybe not, and if he has no wife—"

"I'll try to eat."

"That's my girl."

But she was right. David might make up with her and ruin any chance they had of adopting Hamish. What was he going to do?

Back around the corner and down the hall, in Andrea's room, Brad slumped in a pale green wicker chair. Beth, her back against the wall, stood close to the door. Andrea, her face suffused with anger, lurched up and down the room and stumbled over a rug. Sharp cracks like rifle shots echoed from the forest beyond. The gale howled and rattled the windows.

"Sit down, Mom, before you fall and break a hip."

Andrea tottered over to another chair and lowered her round body to the paisley cushion. Her ancient perfume wafted from her.

What was that she wore? Something she bought from a woman who came to the house.

"Mom, do you need me? If not, I'm going."

"Why would I need you? Go."

Beth slammed the door behind her. Andrea shook her head.

"How did they kill her in prison?"

"How did who kill her?"

"David and Vanessa. Now they're the ones who will adopt Hamish."

"They got Hamish. The court gave them custody."

"They were granted temporary custody until the appeals were finished."

That was clever. Sometimes, Mom brought some sense up from the depths of her alcohol-soaked brain.

"I thought it was done when I signed off."

"Grandparents have rights, too, the lawyer said."

"You think they arranged her overdose."

"Yes."

"Doesn't sound like David."

"She's a bitch. She doesn't like children."

"But she wants David and all that lovely money, and she'll do anything for it. She'll make up with him, and then they'll cut off access. They'll prove you're a drunk in court."

"Don't say that."

"We can hope the wedding's off."

That was the only hope to climb out of the deep well of debt Karen left him in. Defending her in court took every penny he had. No help from David, though it was his father who knocked her up and made her go nuts. Lost his house. But if they had Hamish, the trust would pay for a place for him to live, a decent place, like this lodge.

"Those are pre-wedding jitters, and so long as they're both alive, we have no hope. When the weather clears, I'm going home. No hope at all."

She stumbled from the chair and collapsed on the bed. Brad

stood and loomed over her. Her pale blue eyes, rimmed in red and dripping with tears, peered up at him. What was that in her eyes? Was she afraid of him?

"Perhaps they'll have an accident on the road. You never know, Mom. Don't give up."

Beth braced herself against the door of her mother's room. Rejected again, she thought. Her entire life. What had she said? *Why should I need you?*

She raced down the hall to their room, opened the door and slammed it behind her.

"Wha—," said Kevin.

"Can we get out of here? I can't stay here with her and her favourite child."

"Who?"

"Mom, of course. Who else?"

Hot, furious tears rolled down her face. She swiped them away and fell into an armchair. Behind her, the storm rattled the window, and she shivered as a gust of cold air hit her back. "And why did you open the window? It's freezing outside."

"Had a smoke and you know what David's like."

She lowered the sash on the window and turned the lock. "I want to go home."

"So do I, but there's no way now. What's up with your mother now? Didn't Brad settled her down?"

"Brad? He's useless and as big a drunk as she is. Karen's dead and I suspect she thinks they have no chance of getting Hamish."

"Getting Hamish?"

"Oh, for God's sake, Kevin. That's all she and Brad want. She because she loves the little guy, I guess and he because of all the lovely money in the trust fund."

Beth wandered over and snuggled under his arm. What a strong guy he was, not like her snivelling brother. She leaned over and kissed him.

"The court's not likely to award him to the family of the woman who killed his father," Kevin said.

He pulled her down beside him on the bed.

"You never know. Courts make strange decisions in child custody cases."

"Would you want—"

"God, no. If we wanted kids, we would have our own. We can barely support ourselves in New York, much less two kids."

"Two?"

"I suppose they would go together, but again, you never know."

"Separating them would be cruel."

"Worse things have happened."

"Would their trust money follow them, no matter who adopted them?"

"Sure. The money is for the kids' upkeep and education. That includes paying mortgages, food, extra activities, all that sort of thing."

"And together they would be ready-made family for someone."

"Yeah, David. But as you say, we could have our own."

"Yes."

She rolled towards him and waited.

Chapter Six

Loud voices echoed down the hallway and into Anne and Thomas's room. Anne looked up from her book, and Thomas stirred from his nap.

"What was that?" he said.

"Fighting. I think it's Vanessa and David."

Thomas climbed out of bed and hugged her. "They should keep their door closed."

"We could open ours?"

"Nosy."

"Yes, but I have a bad feeling about this place, maybe because of last year, and I want to understand all these relationships. There's an undercurrent—"

She opened the door a little, but stepped back. Thomas edged in beside her.

"Why do you want rid of the children and the dogs?"

That was David, Anne thought. She'd never heard his voice so full of anger except when his father was killed. But he must be talking to Vanessa. Who else would want to get rid of the children and the dogs?

Vanessa answered, her voice coarse and scornful, "I told you I didn't say that. That little bitch is a liar."

"She never lied before. You don't like the dogs or the children."

"The children, the children. Do you never think about anything else? Why didn't you ask the minister to come yesterday?"

Anne raised her eyebrows at Thomas and opened her mouth to speak, but he put his fingers to his lips. The conversation came closer.

"Where are you going? Stay here. You knew the storm was coming. You're the one who wants rid of me."

"Stop grabbing me, Vanessa. I need to help Mike with the wood. Don't be ridiculous. You wanted to send the dogs out into the storm. They would have died."

Footsteps in the hallway came closer, and she eased the door closed. The fight continued outside their room.

"Smelly beasts."

"What did you say?"

Vanessa's voice changed to a strident whine.

"I said they were smelly beasts and yes, they'll go and the needy, messy children and their simpering nanny with them."

"No."

"No."

Her voice rose to a shriek.

"How can I live with things I loathe? You don't love me. You've never loved me."

Hard to go back from that, Anne thought.

"And perhaps you never loved me. We'll talk this over later."

David must have raced off, Anne thought. One word came through the door.

"Bastard."

Anne raised her eyebrows at Thomas and grimaced.

"Whew."

"Good thing the minister didn't arrive."

"Yes. Should we go down? I think I better see what's in the freezer to feed everyone. Matters will only worsen if they're hungry."

Beth bolted upright and shook Kevin, but he mumbled and shifted away. She shook him again. Would the man ever wake up? He could sleep through a hurricane.

She slipped out of bed and dug her toes into the soft rug. The battle outside the door continued. "Kevin, wake up. Listen to that."

"What?"

"Fighting outside in the hall."

He rubbed the sleep away from his face and shook his head. His voice was still drowsy. Why did it take him so long to wake up? "What? Who's fighting? What kind of fighting?"

"Wake up, Kevin. David and Vanessa. Fighting about the kids."

She threw on her bathrobe and moved closer to the door. The voices carried through from the hallway, clearer now. "They're fighting about the dogs and Eloise, too." "Why are you whispering? They can't hear us with the racket they're making. A lovers' quarrel or—"

"Or, I'd say. That was basic stuff. If David won't give up the kids for her, he's not giving them up at all. Mom and Brad can litigate all they want."

"Are they still in court?"

"Yes, I think so. That's what Mom said."

Kevin threw off the duvet and winced as his feet hit the floor. "Getting cold in here and now I'm hungry. Let's go down and see what's going on and if there's any food."

Beth dressed, and together they walked down the main stairs into the living room and into the kitchen.

Mike hauled logs across the ice-covered snow to the furnace on a red sleigh he found in the woodshed. Someone was thinking ahead. He stoked up the fire and walked back towards the house. Inside, he hung his coat on the pine rack and opened the door to the kitchen.

Trevor stood with his back to him at the counter in front of the toaster.

"Making lunch, are you?" Mike said. "I'm starving."

"Not yet. I'm getting my wife something."

"Say, is your wife ill? She's kind of pale and weak."

"She hasn't been able to eat since she lost our baby."

"That's too bad."

Trevor grabbed a package of arrowroot cookies from the shelf and opened the fridge to take out milk.

"Should we save the milk for the kids? Who knows how long we'll be stuck here?"

"I didn't think."

Trevor poured a glass of orange juice instead and walked back up the stairs with the drink and two cookies.

Anne opened the swinging doors.

"Hi, Mike. Here we are on kitchen duty again."

"Not me. I'm keeping the furnace going."

"Can you plug the furnace into the generator? How's the wood supply?"

"Supply's good. I'm worried about the generator, though. The gas is getting low."

"I thought David had several tanks."

"Delivery next Monday."

"We can keep the wood stove on in here. I'm going to check the freezer."

A walk-in freezer, disguised as a pantry, stood beside the double-wide refrigerator. Inside, Anne took out a stack of pies labelled tourtière. Another bin contained dinner rolls. She took several packages of chicken thighs and set them on top of the fridge to thaw. She was thorough, Mike thought. Last time she organized the food, too.

"Lots of food," she said.

She put the two pies in the oven of the stove and the frozen buns in the warming oven, and then made a dressing, whisking oil into a mixture of vinegar and something else. Garlic, from the smell.

"Who cleared the dining room table?" she said.

"Eloise after the kids were asleep. I think David helped her. Say is something going on there?"

"I have no idea."

She looked as though she did know. Maybe no wedding, ever. That would put Van over the top, and the woman had a temper. What a mess she'd made.

After lunch, the leaden skies outside darkened the living room as though it were evening. A few lights glowed. The adults sat before the fire, huddled under blankets and throws, even though the furnace still blasted out heat. The wind howled in the chimney and stirred the flames. Anne worked on organizing her family files on her computer.

Vanessa, dressed in a thigh-high, elegant woollen dress in green the colour of spring leaves, wandered past but paused to look over Anne's shoulder. "I thought the internet was down," she said.

"I'm organizing the genealogy files that are downloaded to my programme."

"What's a genealogy file?"

"A record that starts with me and goes back in time to all my ancestors and their descendants other than me. I'll show you if you like."

Vanessa dropped onto a chair beside her, adjusted her legs to their best advantage and inspected the family chart Anne showed her. Anne's nose twitched as Vanessa's heavily-applied scent drifted by.

"Do you do it for other people?"

"Sometimes, although I'm an amateur at this."

"I think David said you did his."

"Only a small portion of it to get him started."

"Could I see it?"

"Ask David."

Vanessa slithered over to David, got a brief nod, and came back to Anne, going through the same leg adjustment. Several pairs of masculine eyes followed her progress across the room and into her chair.

"He said yes."

"Okay. It starts here, with David. When I go up one generation, we find his father, Cooper Thwaite and Cooper's mother, Enid.

She was born in 1920 in Yorkshire and had a liaison with an American during the war who died in 1945. Her child was born in 1946. That was Cooper.

His grandfather, Edward Thwaite, a wealthy farmer, raised Cooper when his mother died young. When his grandparents passed away, he took his inheritance to Canada and started a real estate company, building houses in the early 70s. He was a successful, honest businessman, but had an unfortunate tendency to leave women with his children outside of marriage. He did pay for his children, though. He was killed last year by Karen Barrington."

"What do you mean he paid for his children?"

"He has some children that David cares for—Hamish, Olivia, Nicholas who is seventeen and away at school, and he always looked after David."

"What if there were others?"

"Others?"

"That he didn't know or care about."

What a strange question? Perhaps she was an adopted child and found this painful.

"If he didn't know about them, he couldn't care for them."

"Or he just didn't care."

So angry, Anne thought. What did it matter to her?

"The man I knew cared for everything he had responsibility for."

"Could you find others?"

"Through genealogy? Only if I had a starting point. Otherwise, no. You'd need a professional genealogist and likely DNA to do that."

"What about their care? Does David handle all the money?"

"I have no idea, and it's none of my business, Vanessa."

"Fine."

Vanessa floated up, adjusted her dress and stalked away.

No thanks for the lesson, Anne thought. What was she getting at?

"What was that all about," said Thomas, sitting down beside her and peering at the screen.

"Fishing. She wants to learn about David's genealogy. And his money."

Eloise brought the children down the stairs, the two dogs trailing after them. The poodle ran over to Anne and nuzzled her, the other to Thomas.

Across the room, David picked up both children.

"Uncle David, can we play here with the people. We're lonely upstairs," said Olivia.

"Certainly you—"

"Of course not, Olivia. You know this room is for grown-ups only. What were you thinking, Eloise? Take them and those filthy dogs to the kitchen. And put the dogs outside," said Vanessa.

"It's still storming."

"Why do they have a kennel if not for this situation? Dogs belong outside."

"The children may play here for an hour or so, Eloise, as long as they're quiet," said David.

"Then I won't be," Vanessa said and flounced up the stairs.

"Does she hate dogs?" Andrea asked David.

"Only inside."

The dogs in question lay quietly at Anne and Thomas's feet.

"They're such well-behaved dogs," Anne said to Thomas.

"She's pushing David away. First the fight and now this again. I wonder why?"

"Perhaps she's changed her mind."

"Doubtful. Where did everyone go?"

Only Anne, Thomas, David, Eloise and the children remained in the living room. Soon the children were playing, and the adults were talking over fresh coffee.

"David, may we ask what's going on? Is your wedding still on?" said Anne.

David's generous mouth turned down, and a frown darkened his eyes and creased his forehead. "I have no idea."

Eloise lowered her head but not before Anne caught a secret and delighted smile. At that moment, the lights went out, and the minimal sound of the blower for the furnace stopped.

"I'd better find Mike," David said.

Anne scrabbled in her purse, found the miniature flashlight she carried on vacations, and walked into the kitchen. A tiny green light on a powerful lantern with a large battery and the option to perform as a lamp glowed on the bottom shelf of the pantry. She grabbed it and joined the others in the living room. Eloise's sweet voice sang a French lullaby and David lit candles on the mantle. Anne's lantern brightened the room.

"Good idea, Anne. I forgot about them."

"Them? I found one in the pantry."

"Three more in the closet in the mudroom. I'll pull out one of them, and you can take the kids upstairs to play, Eloise."

A now-familiar shriek echoed from upstairs, calling for David.

"I better take one to her too," he said and helped Eloise to take the children upstairs.

"How can he put up with her?" Thomas said.

"I wonder if he is?"

"Is putting up with her? She'd drive me to distraction."

They walked to their room and settled down, Thomas for a nap and Anne with a book. Anne watched his quiet breathing. How comfortable she was with him. What was keeping her from committing to a life with him? It couldn't be just her dislike of living in the United States. She focussed on her book, *Warlight* by Michael Ondaatje, an exploration of family and loss disguised as a post-war thriller set in the fifties. Family and loss. That was the theme of their weekend, too, she thought.

Chapter Seven

Outside, David crunched across the ice-covered snow, at times crashing through. Frozen slush found its way into his boots, soaked his socks, and froze his toes. He reached Mike at the generator that stood near the out-door furnace, a miniature black shed with dials instead of a front door. Mike's parka was coated with ice, his hands encased in yellow work gloves as he checked the motor.

"What's happened, Mike? The ice, or what?"

"I thought it was water or ice in the line, but I checked the propane tanks, and we're down to empty."

David shook his head. What were they going to do now? Vanessa would be wild.

"No delivery this week and we've been using too much."

Mike's ruddy face and light-brown eyebrows were encrusted with snow.

"What now?"

"We'll use the stove and fireplaces and the oil lamps. I have several electric lanterns with high-capacity batteries too. I'll go search them out if you'll start on the wood."

"Yeah. If you see Thomas or Brad, send them out too."

"Will do."

Mike gathered up an armload of wood, breathed in the scent of cut cedar and paper birch, and stomped his way to the kitchen. He piled the logs on the porch and went in. Eloise stood at the counter, putting cookies and milk on a tray. What a lovely woman she was. He could see why Van wanted rid of her. Lots of competition for her when David realized what she was like. If the weather settled in, that would be soon.

"Hi, Eloise."

"Hi. Do we have enough wood?"

"Yes, for now."

"I'll have to bring the children down here to play."

A bit of tension there.

"We'll keep the fireplace going upstairs if you want. You worried about her highness?"

"Yes. Olivia is old enough to understand what she says."

"Poor kid. But David won't let her get away with it. I think they're on the outs."

"On the outs?"

"Not getting along. Is there anything to eat?"

"Bien sûr. Food is left from lunch— tourtière, not too bad and some rolls. I can put it in the oven for you."

"Thanks. Let me know if you need wood for the fireplace in your rooms. We can keep it warm for the kids."

"Merci."

Eloise carried her tray of cookies and milk upstairs.

Yeah, Van was right to be worried about that one.

Much later in the afternoon, Anne left a dozing Thomas, threw on a heavy Icelandic sweater of black and white wool, and took the back stairs to the kitchen. Outside, the rain pelted down, freezing as it hit the stems and branches of the trees, turning shrubs into miniature glass sculptures. How much ice, she wondered. In 1998, the Ottawa Valley and Montreal saw one hundred millimetres of freezing rain that brought down power lines and century-old pines, stranded people in their homes behind live wires across their driveways, and left them in the cold and dark. Successive storms crept in with slow monotonous rain that froze and didn't thaw for days.

This storm raged and howled, and the rain still fell, coating everything in its path. No way to hear a forecast, to know how long the storm would last, or how thick the ice would grow.

People still had to eat, she thought. Ice or no ice. With the generator off, she'd use the more perishable food first, especially the chicken, to avoid illness-causing bacteria. If she didn't open the freezer too often, it should keep most things safe for two days at least. And there was always outside if the temperature fell low enough, but it needed to be below eighteen celsius to freeze. Only minus four to replicate a fridge though. Some things could be kept outside, in a shed perhaps.

With the chicken thawed, she coated it with olive oil and Italian seasoning she found in another section of the pantry, the shelves arrayed with glass and plastic containers of herbs and spices. Whoever cooked here took her craft seriously. Was cooking a skill or an art? In her own case, a utilitarian skill learned from necessity after Michael died. He loved to cook and made all their meals.

She smiled at the memory of him, outfitted with an apron that proclaimed he was Number One in the Kitchen. So many years ago, so much happiness. Had she found the same with Thomas?

She stoked the fire in the white enamel wood stove, added a fresh piece of log to the box, and closed the grate. She popped a frozen cake in the warming oven and waited until the gauge on the roasting oven below steadied at 400F. That should do it, she thought, for the chicken and the potatoes.

She peeled carrots, tossed them with oil and salt and paper and put them on another rack in the oven.

A search of the fridge revealed lettuce and other salad items but no dressing. A vinaigrette would have to do.

She was whisking olive oil into a mixture of red wine vinegar, garlic, and Dijon mustard when Eloise and the children tramped down the stairs. The children wore sweaters atop their miniature turtleneck shirts, Olivia in deep blue and Hamish in bright red. Eloise took off the sweaters and hung one on the back of a chair and the other on the highchair before settling the children in front of quiet toys, colouring for Olivia and several plastic cars for Hamish.

"Can I help, Anne."

"Thanks. Could you feed the dogs? I haven't found their food yet, and they're beginning to resent it."

"Haven't they shown you?"

Eloise pulled on a cupboard handle which tilted out to reveal a bin full of kibble.

"I wondered why they stared at that corner."

"Should I set the table in here or the dining room?"

"The dining room if we can warm it enough."

"David lit the fire a while ago, I think."

"How are you?"

Eloise's dark eyes searched Anne's.

"You know, don't you?"

"Yes. I imagine most people know. Love lights up your face."

"He doesn't see it. He only sees her."

"Not so much. We'd better get on."

Eloise shot her a perplexed glance, gathered a tray full of plates and cutlery, and swung through the door to the dining room. Experienced, Anne thought. She hasn't always been a nanny. And so in love.

Anne woke Thomas, who dressed in his usual rapid fashion and a few minutes later, came down the stairs into the dining room. She placed hand-thrown ceramic bowls of pickles and olives on the table and cast a discerning eye around the room. Candles in antique brass sticks marched down the centre of the dining room table. On the sideboard, ruby-shaded lamps burning scented oil lent a fragrance of pine woods and a glow of sunset to the scene. Carafes of white and red wine sparkled in front of them. Drapes on the window, in shades of dusty rose and deep blue, shuttered the storm away.

He enfolded her in his arms, and she leaned back into his embrace.

"Is this your work?"

"No, Eloise arranged it."

Off to the side, the children sat with Eloise at a card table set with white kitchen china.

"Eloise, would you like to join us?" David said when he sat down at the head of the table.

"I'm sure she's happier with the children. They are her job," said Vanessa.

Arrayed tonight in a full-length black gown, its plunging neckline filled with a cascade of diamonds, she pouted at David when he asked again.

"Eloise?"

"Thank you, I'll stay here. Hamish needs help with his meat, and Olivia likes company."

Andrea and Brad came down the stairs. She stumbled on a scatter rug, but he grabbed her. A stray lock of grey hair escaped from the chignon affected at the back of her head and trailed across her shoulder. She also wore a formal gown, emerald green with a high neck and capped sleeves. Perhaps she should have too, Anne thought, aware of her casual shirt and jeans.

"You don't need to be so rough," Andrea said.

"You're not a lightweight, Mom."

They, too, sat at the end of the table, Andrea to David's right and Brad to his left. When Beth and Kevin came down, neither in formal dress, they took seats as far from Andrea and Brad as they could. No family love there, Anne thought.

Opposite David, Vanessa sulked behind her wine glass. The light from the lamp stained her hair to a faint pink.

"Trevor, I'd like some more red wine," she asked.

He raised his eyebrows but went to the sideboard with her glass. Why the questioning look? Perhaps she didn't drink a great deal, Anne thought. But how would he know?

Back in his own seat, Trevor encouraged Carmel to eat, speaking to her in soothing tones, as one might a restless child. Her eyes focussed on Hamish, Anne noticed. She nodded to Mike, they went to the kitchen and carried in the chicken and vegetables, and sat.

The children finished; Eloise brought them to say goodnight to David and the company, and they returned to the nursery.

"What are we going to do, David? Andrea said.

Slurring her words again, Anne thought, watching Andrea refill her glass from the bottle that stood between her and Brad. Brad was drinking steadily too.

"About what?"

"The lack of food, the heat, the power, the damned ice," said Brad.

"There's lots of food and wood. We ran out of fuel for the generator, but we have candles and lamps."

"I want to get out of here," Andrea said.

"Depends on the storm."

"What about the snowmobiles?" said Brad.

"Not too good on ice and we don't know what the trails are like now. Lots of downed trees," said Mike.

Andrea's voice rose to a grating wail, and tears overflowed her blood-shot eyes.

"We're trapped."

"No, we're not trapped, Andrea. We have to wait until the storm is over and we can make sure there's no danger from power lines and trees. Have patience," said Thomas.

Andrea subsided, drank from her glass, and poured more wine. The neck of the bottle chattered on the crystal, and red wine spilled over, staining the white table cloth.

An image rose in Anne's mind of blood oozing from the body of the boy she'd found years before in Bermuda, and she shivered.

"Anne?" said Thomas.

"Nothing."

Beth hurried to the kitchen, came back with a few paper towels, and mopped up the mess, whispering to her mother the whole time. The lid of the stove crashed after she went into the kitchen. The sherry-like odour of the burning, wine-soaked paper drifted into the room when she returned.

Andrea and Brad murmured to each other, Vanessa fumed at one end of the table, and Trevor whispered to Carmel. Kevin patted Beth's hand and kissed her lightly on the cheek when she sat down again. A reward for the work or soothing her rage, Anne wondered.

When the meal was over, David raised his glass.

"Well done, Anne," said David. "Thank you so much. A toast to the cook."

"I'm sure anyone can stick chicken and potatoes in the oven," said Vanessa in a loud aside to Trevor.

"In a wood stove?" said David.

"Oh, yes. I forgot Anne was your pet because she found out who killed your beloved father. Some people here wish she hadn't; don't they, Andrea?"

"Vanessa, be quiet."

"No. She ruined everyone's life with her prying and poking."

"Karen murdered a man," said Thomas.

"What a man. Look at the poor bastard children and you, David, and how many more? He was revolting."

Vanessa shoved her chair backwards, crashing it to the wall behind and raced up the stairs.

"I'll make sure she's okay," said David. "The wine hit her."

"Maybe it would be better if someone else—"

"I don't think so."

A few minutes later, he plodded down the stairs.

"She says she's going to bed."

Soon the dining room emptied. Brad took Andrea upstairs, Kevin and Beth followed, as did Trevor and Carmel.

Anne cleared her plate and cutlery and Thomas's from the table. He followed her out with two more.

"How long?" Anne said.

"Two days. Sooner, if the cell service comes back."

"My phone is dying."

"Mine too. David didn't mention a satellite phone?"

"Not to me."

Mike and David carried more dishes into the kitchen and returned.

"David, you don't have a sat phone here, I suppose?" said Anne.

"We did. I kept it on the hall table, but it disappeared yesterday."

"Someone took it. How odd? Perhaps Olivia?" said Thomas.

"She's a bit of a rascal, but she hasn't bothered the phones before. I'll ask her in the morning."

A few minutes later, Anne walked into the kitchen to find Beth at the sink, elbow-deep in suds.

"Did you get hot water from the stove?" Anne asked.

"Yes. Someone said that you did all the work last time, and I remembered it was true. I'm so sorry I didn't help you more then but I will this time."

"Thanks. Mike helped a lot, but he's on wood detail this time."

Finished, Beth sat at the table, her hands clenched white.

"What—"

"Don't you feel it? Someone is so angry."

"Vanessa."

"Yes, but she left the room and the feeling of—I don't know, hidden rage maybe—was still there."

"Are you sensitive to atmosphere? I must admit, other than watching the drinking and Vanessa's anger, I didn't notice much."

"Something underneath. I'd like to go up."

She swung the door to the living room and came back.

"Kevin's gone to our room. Would you come to the top of the stairs with me?"

"Of course, but why do you think you are in more danger than I?"

"It's my family. My mother is so irrational."

"Come on. I'll go upstairs with you to your room. Kevin is there by now and you'll be safe. I'm sure we all are."

Eloise poked at the embers of the fire when they returned to the nursery. The fire had raced through the logs she added before dinner.

"Olivia, I'm going downstairs for some more wood. Don't wake Hamish."

"I won't."

Eloise gathered up an armload of wood in the kitchen and carried it back to the nursery. Hamish slept on in his crib, but Olivia was nowhere to be seen. She checked the bathrooms and the one empty room. What a child. Perhaps she went downstairs. She liked Anne.

Eloise raced down the stairs to the kitchen and burst through the door, sending it crashing back into the wall.

"What's the matter?" said Anne.

"Have you seen Olivia?"

"She hasn't been down here."

"She couldn't have gone out?"

"No, no. Not this way."

Eloise ran into the living room, empty now of the guests. David stood in the bow window, peering out at the storm.

"David, David."

"What?"

"Has Olivia been down here?"

"No. She can't have gone outside, Eloise. We'll find her. You know how she likes to explore the lodge. You go back upstairs, and I'll check the basement."

Olivia tiptoed over the crib. Hamish had his dinosaur pyjamas on with his bum sticking up in the air like always. She crept away and out the door. There was no one in the hallway. She hurried down the hall to Vanessa's room. The door was open, and Vanessa wasn't there either. Maybe she could put the paper back before Vanessa knew she took it.

But shoes clicked on the hall floor. She ran to the closet, opened the door, and squeezed behind the long dresses. She better not touch them or Vanessa would be really mad. The closet smelled like Vanessa. She didn't like it. She liked how Eloise smelled, like the outside in the garden. She stuffed her hands in her pockets and waited.

When Vanessa came in, someone came with her.

"What brought that on."

That was Uncle David, but he sounded so cross. Why was he cross with Vanessa?

"Leave me alone."

"This isn't going to work, Vanessa."

"What?"

Vanessa sounded cross like she did when she said she would spank.

"The dogs, the children, even the lodge. You don't want to share my life; you want to destroy it."

"You bastard. I gave up my career for you."

"What career? A few photographs in a minor magazine."

Eloise heard something crash, and then the door opened and closed. Eloise listened. Did they both go? What could she do?

Someone rapped at the door.

"What is it?"

"Vanessa, have you seen Olivia."

That was Eloise.

"No, and the brat isn't in here."

For a long time, she stood behind the dresses and waited. After a while, Vanessa snored. Olivia giggled. Maybe she could leave now. She edged out but the door to the hall opened, and she hid again. Someone crossed the room and was quiet, and then went.

Olivia crept out of the closet. Why was Vanessa's cover all red? She looked like she was sleeping. Now she was scared. If Vanessa woke up, she would blame her for putting red paint on her clothes. She scurried to the door and looked down the hall. A man turned the corner. Who was that? She raced back to the playroom. Eloise wasn't there, and Hamish was still sleeping. She curled up in a chair. She was tired now too.

Eloise came back and picked her up and rocked her.

"Where did you go, Olivia?"

She better not say she was in Vanessa's room.

"I wanted to see the other bathroom."

"Why?"

"Sometimes there are pretty bottles."

"You are such a magpie."

"What is a magpie?"

"A bird that collects shiny things. Go to sleep now."

Eloise rocked and sang a little song that made Olivia feel safe.

A few minutes later, she slept.

Downstairs, David shone a powerful flashlight into the wine cellar and cedar closet, inhaling the woodsy scent before he went on the mechanical room and storage. He checked behind boxes and crates of old possessions and luggage, but there was no sign of the little girl. She was so inquisitive and fearless, she could be anywhere. But not outside, he reassured himself. She wouldn't go outside. Perhaps she was back in the nursery by now.

He climbed the stairs to the kitchen and on up.

In the hallway, Eloise stood with her back to the door of the children's room, her head turned away from him.

When he came up to her, he whispered her name.

"She's back," Eloise said. "She's asleep now."

David hugged her and stepped back, conscious of overstepping the boundaries he'd made for himself.

"I'm sorry, Eloise. I was so worried."

"That's okay. Olivia said she went to the hall bathroom to look for pretty bottles. I hope that's all she was doing. She's restless with no outside play these last two days."

"I hope not in Vanessa's—"

"Non. When I rapped on the door, she said that Olivia wasn't there."

"Good. I'll talk to Olivia in the morning."

Chapter Eight

The next morning, Anne shifted in bed to look at the time and the scene outside. The wind had died in the night, and filtered sunshine slipped through the windows, spilled across the floor, and dappled the bed. The ice didn't coat the glass on this side of the house. Outside the landscape of a frozen planet loomed—misshapen, wounded trees, wires coated in ice lying on the ground, crab apples, their red skin visible under two inches of ice, and everywhere stillness. Sunshine scattered through twigs of ice as though a chandelier hung in the sky. She smiled and slipped out of bed for a closer look. Lovely, but deadly, she thought.

"Thomas, the storm is over."

He moaned and covered his head. "What's the time?"

"Seven. I'm going down to start breakfast."

"We should talk."

"I—"

"We must."

What could she say to him? She loved him, but she couldn't live with him in the USA, become a citizen, even in Vermont, much as she liked Culver's Mills. What could they do? What would he do?

"I want to marry you. I'm tired of roaming around, unattached, with no home, no one to return to."

"I want to marry you. I love you and want to spend my life with you. But not in the USA. Not now."

"The President's time will end."

"But the people who voted for him, the people who go armed and think that's okay, the people who think babies should be ripped from their mothers' breasts will still be there. I can't live among them. I can't."

"I'm an American. You have American friends."

"Yes, I do. People I love dearly, but half, half of the people voted for that man."

Anne twisted away and out of bed to pace the room. Sunshine crept through the window and shattered on the carpet.

"Do you want to live in Toronto."

She glanced at him and smiled. Toronto. Perhaps. "Would you do that? What about your home in Vermont? What about the grandchildren? What about your business?"

"No reason we can't visit?"

"That depends on how things are going, doesn't it. You know the fascist turn the government is taking."

"The election—"

"Perhaps. Perhaps he won't be reelected. And what about you? Are you on his enemies list?"

"Not yet. And is Ontario much better with that—? Politics shouldn't govern our life. Is that all this is? The politics?"

"So much has happened—from Vermont to Bermuda to Spain. I'm still working through all that and the fear."

Two murders in Vermont, one in Bermuda that almost imprisoned her, a race with a vulnerable child across Europe, and then the attempt to murder her in Vermont. And Karen's attempt on her life in this very building. Too much death and too much fear.

"Come here."

She snuggled back into bed and into his arms.

"We belong together. So long as we agree on that, the rest is logistics."

She caressed his stubbled face. His dark eyes, crinkled at the margins, full of love, watched her face.

"We belong together, but—"

Disappointment fell across his face and shuttered his eyes. She stroked his face again but, after a moment, wriggled out of his embrace and climbed out of bed.

"Give me another day or so. Meanwhile, people have to be fed."

"Another day. They have to be fed by you?"

"And Eloise. Another woman trying to make a decision."

"Is she?"

"She loves David."

"And he?"

"Beginning to, I think."

His voice, full of sadness and not a little impatience, reached her in the bathroom. "You're so good with other people's relationships. Bring some of that insight to ours. I'm tired of waiting for your decision."

She peered around the doorframe towards him. "I know. Please. A little more time."

No one screaming. No one calling for help. Why hadn't someone discovered her?

The killer crept off the bed and stood at the window. The storm was over, but from the thick ice covering the downed power lines, no one would be leaving soon. Good. He had more work to do. He sat down at a pine desk fitted into a corner of the room, and composed a note, printing in careful block letters. That should frighten that nosy pair, keep them from interfering in what had to be done.

Anne stirred the embers in the wood stove, added some kindling and a sturdy log, peeling some of the white bark and adding it to the growing fire. She moved the green-enamelled kettle to the burner and left it to bubble away to itself.

Eloise opened the door from the stairwell. Dark circles shadowed her eyes, and her usually happy mouth turned down. A sleepless night, Anne supposed.

"Morning, Eloise. The storm is over."

"Dieu merci. Perhaps everyone will relax a little."

"One can only hope."

Eloise sat at the table with a hand on her forehead. When Anne spoke, she lifted her dark eyes to meet Anne's. Troubled, Anne thought. Why? "Do you have a headache?"

"Non. I am worried about Olivia. She has a cauchemar, crying and sobbing. When I woke her, she begged me not to spank her. No one ever spanks her, and I don't know where she heard the word. And she was missing for an hour, hiding somewhere I suppose. Sometimes she plays games by herself."

"A nightmare. Does Olivia spend time with her mother?"

"No, no. Her maman dumped Olivia at David's door two years ago and later died in a car accident. He went to the court, and now he is the guardian."

Anne poured boiling water into the family-sized Italian coffee maker. "Perhaps Vanessa?"

"Perhaps. When she wakes up, I will ask her about the dream."

"She may not remember."

Anne poured cups for them both and then filled another as a gust of cold wind from the outside door brought Mike into the kitchen with an armload of wood.

"Thanks, Mike. I'll need to feed the stove soon."

"Let me. She's melting outside, eh. Coffee. Great."

He reached for a mug and wrapped his hands around it.

"That's good news. Did you go down the lane?"

"As far as I could but the hydro pole is down across it, and the wires may be live. Some trees beyond it are down too. Lots of chainsawing before we can get out."

"There'll be some unhappy people here this morning."

"Why will people be unhappy?" Trevor said as he and Carmel walked in from the living room.

"The road is still impassable."

"You came in a helicopter. Will it come back for you?"

"Not for two days unless the cell service comes back on or David finds the satellite phone."

Beth and Kevin came next, looking carefree and cheerful in ski sweaters and jeans. Behind them, David came down the stairs. Darkness surrounded his eyes and fatigue marked his face.

"Bad night?" said Anne.

"Not much sleep."

Anne fried bacon in the black iron pan and put the plate in the warming oven. She found an antique toaster, sliced bread and put the toaster in the oven. On the stove top, coffee bubbled in a white percolator, a jaunty blue cornflower decorating its side. One percolator wasn't going to do it this morning, she thought. She refilled the Italian carafe with more water and added eggs to her pan.

"Where's Thomas," said David.

"Still sleeping. I'll go up when the eggs are done. What about Vanessa?" said Anne.

"I haven't seen her yet. She's not too sociable without her coffee."

"I'll take her some on my way. How does she take it?"

"Black."

The door to Vanessa's room stood ajar. Anne raised her fist to knock when a ray of light, passing through a chink in the curtains, crossed the carpet and fell across the object on the bed.

"Vanessa," she said.

When there was no response, Anne pushed aside the door with mounting dread, found a place for the coffee on a dresser and flicked on the light. The object turned into Vanessa's body, its arm hanging off the bed, its abdomen soaked with blood. Slashes in her silk nightgown. A knife then. Vanessa's lovely eyes, blank and clouded, stared at nothing. No horror on the face. Had she been sleeping and woke only as the knife plunged into her? Or did she not wake at all until death took her. A metallic smell of blood, but not the other, darker stench of death. It wouldn't be long for that.

What should she do? What would they all do now?

She reached forward, staying as far away as possible, and touched the forehead with the back of her hand. Deadly cold. Her fingers found nothing where a pulse should be. It would be hours or days until the police would come. She shouldn't touch it, but someone would ask if the body was stiff. She lifted the arm from the bed, tried to flex the wrist and the elbow. Stiff. She checked the feet. Fully established rigor. The room was cool but not cold. She should take a room temperature.

What else? Time. She checked her watch. 8:30 am, but she wouldn't be the one to fill out the certificate. Not this time. Blood rushed with the sound of blowing sand through her head. She must get out before she fainted all over the crime scene. At the door, she took the coffee with her.

Outside, she sank to the floor, gulped the coffee, and put her head down to her knees. Footsteps neared her, and a rush of fear swept over her.

"What are you doing, Anne? Are you sick?"

Thomas. It was Thomas. He squatted down beside her and put his arm around her. She rested her head on his shoulder for a moment and took a deep breath. "Vanessa is dead. Stabbed, I think. Blood everywhere."

"What the hell? Who?"

"Vanessa."

"Who would kill her?"

Thomas took his arm back, held her face for a moment with concern in his eyes, stood, and pushed open the door. He looked down at her, a question in his eyes. "What?"

"Why did you go in?"

"Why? What does it matter? I did, and there the body lay, like all the others. Why are you questioning me?"

Thomas backed away, his hands up. He needed to know.

"I'm sorry. The door was ajar. I saw Vanessa in the light from the window when I was bringing her coffee."

Her tongue stuck to the roof of her mouth, and she shivered again. She reached a hand up to Thomas. "Help me up. We've got to tell the rest."

"Can you stay here? I'll get David so we can lock it up."

"We have to turn off the heat in there and take the temperature of the room now and open the windows a crack before—"

"One thing at a time."

Anne sank to the floor again as he left her.

Bodies everywhere she went. Everywhere. How could she go through it again? How? She hid her face in her hands and sobbed.

Chapter Nine

Thomas found David in the kitchen with Mike, sitting at the worn pine table—two friends chatting over breakfast. The comforting smells of bacon and toast mingled with coffee in the warm air from the stove.

"Storm coming back, I think," said Mike.

"Coming back?" said David.

"Yeah. Wind's picking up and the temp's dropping. Ice staying around for a while."

Both looked up when Thomas sat down without a word. He noted the dark circles around David's eyes and the usual happy-go-lucky look Mike wore. No nervous tension that he could see. Could David have made that furious assault on the woman he was supposed to love and not show it? What motive could Mike have to kill a woman he barely knew? Or was that an assumption?

"What's up, Tom?" David said.

"I have bad news—"

Mike laughed, the booming sound filling the room, but stopped when he glanced at Thomas. "Bad news. How did you get any news?" he said.

"It's Vanessa."

"What's —" said David.

"There's no easy way to tell you this. She's dead, David—"

"No. You've made a mistake. Who says she's dead?"

He shoved the table out of his way, sent his chair crashing into the counter, and raced towards the stairs.

"Stop," said Thomas. "Stop, Dave."

David hesitated at the door, his face red with anger. "Why?"

"I'm coming with you."

"So am I," said Mike.

Thomas glanced at Mike. His face was ashen, and tears threatened to break from his eyes. How fond was he of Vanessa? Didn't he just meet her? But there was no time to wonder. David thundered up the stairs and along the hall. Thomas took the stairs two-at-a-time and was at David's heels when he stopped in front of Anne.

"What happened?" David said.

He tried to push past Thomas, who blocked the door and put his hand on David's shoulder. "You can go in, but you can't touch her."

"Why the hell not?"

"Because she was murdered."

Colour drained from David's face, and he staggered into the wall. Mike ran up to them. "Did you say murdered?"

"Yes. Only David goes in, and he only looks."

"But—"

Anne stood up and took Mike's hand. "No, Mike," she said. "Go downstairs and bring me the thermometer from the kitchen wall. I need the temperature in the bedroom.

Inside the room, David shook off Thomas's hand, hid his face, and sobbed.

The copper smell of blood filled the room, and something more, something coming underneath. She'd been dead a while, Thomas thought. David took a step towards the bed.

"No, David."

David, his face suffused with rage, whirled on Thomas, "Why the hell not? Who put you in charge? This is my house. I was going to marry her."

"Everyone's a suspect. You can't touch her."

"A suspect? I loved her."

"Everyone heard your fight with her."

"It was just a fight. Everybody fights."

His rage faded; he whimpered, his eyes pleading with Thomas. "I didn't do this, Tom."

"We have to do all we can to make sure the police can find out who did. I'm going to open the windows in here. Can I trust you to stay away from her?"

"No. I'll go outside."

Thomas pulled the double-hung windows down from the top, and frigid air streamed into the room, replacing the miasma of death. His thoughts turned to Anne. How was she going to handle yet another murder? Last winter in Culver's Mills had been bad enough and almost ended their relationship. Not this time. He wouldn't let it.

Back in the hall, David beat the wall with a slow rhythm. Anne handed the thermometer to Thomas and gripped Mike's hand.

"Are there keys?" Thomas asked.

"Keys?"

"I want to lock the room."

"Yes."

David dug in his pocket and handed a key ring to Thomas. He chose the one that read Vanessa, slipped inside, and waited until the thermometer stopped dropping. Outside again, he locked the door and pocketed the key.

"Sixteen celsius," he said to Anne.

A querulous voice behind him said, "What in heaven's name is going on here?"

Andrea, dressed in jeans and a navy, Irish-knit sweater, stood in the doorway of her room down the hall.

"Go downstairs, Andrea. We're coming down to tell you," David said.

"Don't tell me—"

"Go."

She searched David's face, shrank back, and tottered off towards the stairs.

Anne held Mike's hand until they reached the stairwell, releasing it to follow him down to the kitchen. Behind her, Andrea nattered at Thomas, demanding to know why they were huddled in the hallway outside Vanessa's room. He didn't answer.

The wood stove filled the kitchen with warmth and the sweet scent of burning maple logs. Eloise, her dark hair tied back and her face calm, buttered toast at the counter. New storm clouds, visible through the window over the sinks, dark and heavy with snow, gathered for a fresh assault over the pine trees at the edge of the clearing. Anne shuddered. Would they never escape from this place?

"Where are the children?" David asked.

"Still sleeping."

Brad stood at the open fridge. He carried milk and orange juice to the table, his eyes narrowing when he saw the troubled faces. "What's the matter?" he said.

Thomas, standing at the end of the table, said, "Please, sit down. We have something to tell you."

Andrea sank into the armchair at the head of the table; Eloise slipped into a chair beside David and Brad. Anne sat beside Brad.

"Where are Trevor and Carmel?"

"Here we are," Trevor said, swinging open the door from the living room.

"And Beth and Kevin? Did anyone call them?"

Anne rushed up the stairs, told Beth they were needed in the kitchen, and ran back down to her place at the table.

They arrived, with curiosity and nothing else that Anne could see, on their faces. Everyone waited. Someone held his breath, or so it seemed to Anne. Perhaps they all did. Anne watched Beth's hands, again in that white-knuckled grip. What would she feel this time, with another murder?

"This morning, Anne took Vanessa some coffee on her way to wake me up. Vanessa's door was ajar, and Anne saw her body on the bed," Thomas said.

"Her body? That's a strange way to put it," said Brad.

Thomas, his voice harsh and brutal, said, "Anne found Vanessa dead, stabbed in the gut. Someone here has murdered her."

"No," said Eloise and Brad.

Andrea screamed, a high-pitched sound that threatened to spiral into hysteria, but Brad went to her, put his arms around her and whispered in her ear until she calmed.

Trevor hugged Carmel, who turned her frantic face to him. Beth hid her face in Kevin's sweatshirt. He wrapped his arms around her.

But then, all eyes focussed on Anne. Her face burned, and she fought to open her throat, inclined to close in moments of high stress.

"I went in far enough to touch her forehead and take her pulse. She was dead. Her arms were stiff."

David's nostrils flared, and his face reddened. Veins in his neck popped. "Why could you touch her and not me?"

Anne touched his hand, but he pulled away from her. "Because I'm a doctor and it's my duty."

"How do we know you didn't kill her?" said Andrea.

Again, Anne thought. Someone wanted to accuse her again.

"And why would Anne do that? She met her a few hours ago," Thomas said. "Anne and I know only David, and only because of business and the death last year. Someone stabbed Vanessa, in the abdomen, multiple times. Someone who wanted to make sure she would die. Someone full of rage or despair or hate."

"What are we going to do?" Eloise said.

David started and stared at Eloise as though he had never seen her before. "You are going to care for the children and keep them safe. Can you go up and wait with them until I come? I want to tell Olivia myself."

"Of course."

Eloise walked to the stairs and on up.

"Of course, she hated Vanessa," said Andrea.

His voice savage, David said, "Repeat that and when we're out of here, you'll find yourself on the wrong end of a suit for slander and cut off from Hamish."

Andrea shrank back, her face ageing in seconds, and turned in a panic to Brad.

"Leave my mother alone, or you'll find yourself on the wrong end of my fist," he said.

"Calm down. And if you can't do that, go back upstairs," Thomas said.

"Trevor, take me home. Take me home," Carmel whispered. "I can't stay here."

"We all have to stay," said Thomas. "A new storm is coming."

"Better cart some more wood in."

Pragmatic Mike took his coat from a hook and trudged out to the woodpile. He was hurting, Anne thought, but why?

"I'll join him," said Kevin.

Beth put her hand on his arm but snatched it back when he shook his head at her. "Kev— "

"Wait upstairs and lock your door."

Beth took the back stairs, and the sound of her slammed door echoed down to them.

A fresh onslaught of wind shook the windows as though to emphasize Thomas's words, and snow swirling against the panes hid the landscape.

Silence lengthened. Anne gave David a piece of toast and a cup of strong black tea with sugar, an old remedy for shock and slipped into her seat beside Thomas. What were they going to do? Vanessa's room was secure for now, and the open windows would keep that temperature down, but they would need to move the body outside if they weren't freed soon. David jerked his chair back, stood up, and sat down again. His eyes pleaded with them.

"Can you find out who did it, Tom, Anne?"

Anne felt her body go cold. Not again. They couldn't get involved again. "We're not police," Anne said. "We can't go around demanding people account for their time and so on."

"You did it before."

"Only by accident and only when we were asked," she said.

"I'm asking."

"I mean asked by the police or someone in authority of some kind. We're all suspects. When the police come, they won't want us to ask so many questions that all the stories are set, all alibis formulated."

She looked at Thomas, willing him to support her.

"But we are trapped here with a murderer," Thomas said.

No, oh no. Not him too. She pushed away from the table and leaned against the sink, her back towards them, rigid. "Yes, and if we try to find out who that is, we'll be targets too."

"I'd rather do something," Thomas said.

Of course, he'd rather do something. He'd always rather do something. He trained for this or something like this.

"Remember what happened in Culver's at Christmas."

She recognized the desperation in her own voice and willed herself to be calm, her throat to stay open, and fear not turn into a constricting rope around her neck.

"What happened where?" asked David.

She pulled out her chair and took her place at the table. "In Culver's Mills, Thomas's home town. We arrived for Christmas, but an assassin sent to recover a Fabergé egg tried to kill us."

David's eyes widened, and for a moment, his jaw dropped.

"A Fabergé egg? What the hell? In Vermont? Why?"

"Because I had crossed her before and because she thought I had the egg. She assaulted Thomas. She almost killed him."

Thomas's strong, warm hand grasped hers. "And you. But we weren't."

"We might not be so lucky this time."

"Please, Anne. What about the children? What if this person is attacking people close to me?"

"Who would do that?"

"I don't know. Brad, Andrea, maybe."

The children. Who knew what demented reason caused that ferocious attack on Vanessa, Anne thought. But it was ferocious, and she lay there, not defending herself. She wasn't drunk. Why were there no defensive wounds? Was she drugged? Did she take sleeping pills? Stop questioning, she urged herself.

"We can listen to what people say. And they will talk," said Thomas.

"I have to think about it. I'm going up," said Anne.

She opened the door to the stairwell.

"Anne, please," said David. "Please."

"I want to think."

Upstairs, she felt in her pocket for a tissue and found the note. In block letters, it read *Don't be curious this time or Vanessa won't be the only one.* Who was the killer threatening, her or Thomas, or both of them?

Chapter Ten

When the knock came at the door, Beth tiptoed over and whispered. "Who's there?"

"Me."

Kevin's voice. She rested her forehead on the door, let out a long sigh, and turned the lock. When he came in, she rushed into his arms, breathing in the scent of wood chips from his jacket. His heart was pounding. Why? "Are you—"

"I was afraid you wouldn't answer. We don't know why Vanessa was killed. Perhaps someone is killing young women. I don't know this guy Mike or Trevor for that matter, and who the hell are Thomas and Anne. They seem to have been around a lot of dead bodies."

"Stop, Kevin. Stop. Everyone can't be a killer."

He smoothed her hair away from her forehead. "I'm sorry, baby. As I climbed the stairs in the dark, I terrified myself thinking I would find you dead too."

"But I'm not. And no one has a reason to kill us. We aren't hateful people like Vanessa."

"Hateful?"

"Oh, yes. Several people hated her, beginning with my mother and brother. What if they killed her? What will we do?"

"Come and lie down."

He wrapped her in the cocoon of his arms and murmured against her hair. He always told her how much he loved the scent of her hair. Lemon and sunshine, he said. "No one in your family killed anyone, baby. Karen was an in-law—"

"Trevor is her brother."

"Trevor has his hands full with Carmel's illness. Stop brooding. The storm will end soon, and we can get out of here. Thomas's helicopter will come for them and for us too, or we can drive out if the roads are cleared."

"The police will come and interview us."

"Don't worry about that now. And you have nothing to fear from the police."

What would the police think? How were they going to send word to them? Kevin stroked her shoulders until she relaxed. Soon she would sleep.

Down the hall, David knocked on the door of the playroom and went in. Eloise sat on the pine floor with Hamish who played with his blocks, building them into awkward towers of three or four, knocking them down and laughing his baby laugh. Olivia coloured at her table under the window.

He prepared this room for them, painting the cupboards and open shelves in primary colours, arranging for the curtains made in material that would let in lots of light, carpeting the bare floorboards to keep them warm for little toes and furnishing with a play-table and child-sized chairs. He planned to convert the space to a bedroom for Olivia alone when the children were old enough to sleep apart. "May I come in?"

"Of course."

Her voice was part of the reason he hired her—soft, comforting, with that charming French accent. She was qualified too. A B.A. in art and a B. Ed. Lucky for him teaching was a tough profession to break into. She sat on the mat beside Hamish and hugged the little boy to her. She was graceful, he thought, and she skied and swam and was qualified to teach those skills too.

He drew a schoolroom chair near Olivia and folded himself into it beside her. "Olivia, I have something to tell you."

"A surprise?"

"No, not a surprise. Something sad."

Olivia got up from her chair and stood close to him. She touched his face and snuggled in. "Are you sad, Uncle David?"

"Yes. A bad thing happened to Vanessa. She was badly hurt, and now she's not alive anymore."

"Dead like my kitten?"

Her kitten died of feline leukemia a month before.

"Yes, dead like the kitten."

"Will we bury her in the garden, too."

"No, grownups go to a special place to be buried. That won't happen for a little while. Not until the storm is over."

A shadow passed over the little girl's face. Her brows knitted, and she pouted. "Vanessa didn't like me."

How did she know that? Had she been listening to them fight?

"Did you like her?"

"No. Vanessa said she would spank me."

"Spank you. Why?"

David shot a glance at Eloise who shrugged and nodded.

"Because I wanted to look at her pretty jewellery."

"Did you go in her room?"

Olivia hung her head and nodded.

"You mustn't touch other people's things."

"I'm sorry. I'm sorry you're sad."

She put up her arms, he picked her up, and she patted his back with her tiny hands. He met Eloise's gaze over the child's head.

"You play with your crayons now," he said as he lowered her to the floor.

"I'm not playing. I'm making art."

David stood up and gestured towards the door to Eloise.

Outside, she said, "I'm so sorry for your loss, David."

Her soft brown eyes looked up into his.

"Thank you. Did you know she threatened to spank Olivia?"

"I knew someone did. She cried about that in her sleep. I was going to talk to you this morning."

"I don't think I really understood her."

"I must return to the children."

He followed her lithe figure as she knelt beside Olivia and whispered to her. Had he ever loved Vanessa or had he been infatuated with the glamour?

He walked down the hall to the room he'd hoped to share Vanessa.

Trevor opened the door to their bathroom to find Carmel, naked, standing on her scale. She travelled with the damn thing everywhere, and no one could use it but her. At home, neither he or the housekeeper moved it so much as a centimetre.

Her ribs made a ladder of her chest, and the sharp wings of her pelvis jutted out from her body. So pale. She plucked at the loose skin over her abdomen. "Look at this, Trevor. I gained more weight. How could I? I've been so good."

Her voice rose in a mournful wail.

"That's not fat, sweetheart. Just loose skin. You've lost more weight."

"The scales are wrong. If I'm fat, they won't let us adopt a baby. I'll never be a mother."

She rushed past him onto the bed. He sat beside her and rubbed her shoulders. More bone. She was almost plump when they married. He loved her curves and her softness, then.

"Perhaps David will let us adopt Hamish now that he won't be married," he said.

She stared at him. Had he been too blunt, too uncaring about a murder?

"He won't. I heard him talking to Anne. He loves the children. He'll never let them go. Never. And even if he did, Brad and Andrea would want Hamish."

So she was looking at it from their point of view, how it would benefit them. Maybe give her some hope, some reason to eat again...

"No, not Andrea. She's a drunk, and the social workers wouldn't let her have him. No, the only obstacle is David. I can talk him around."

Her eyes, swollen with tears over her knife-sharp cheekbones, met his. "You'll talk to him?"

"I will. I want you to be well again."

Mike waited until the kitchen emptied, and Kevin dumped his firewood before coming in with his armload of birch and maple. He stacked the logs in a cast iron bucket beside the stove, ate some breakfast, and remembered the early days with Vanessa. They had fun for a while, but she always wanted money. She always wanted Thwaite money. So sure she was hard done by. So sure Thwaite ignored her on purpose. But that wasn't like Cooper or David. She wouldn't listen when he told her to go to them and tell them who she thought she was. She insisted on doing it her way. When the cops came, they would find out about her and him. What should he do? What could he do?

And should he tell what he saw? That could mean money in his pocket. He needed money. The mortgage was due on the house, and it was her turn to pay. Not happening now.

He wondered if she left a will and if she had anything to leave. Did David give her any money, any real money? He was her heir, not David. There was no one else.

The door opened. Him.

"I wondered when you would come back here. Planning to wipe your fingerprints off the knives. I know what you did, you bastard."

"What do you think I did?"

"You killed her."

"No—"

"Yes. I saw you take the knife."

"Did you tell the others?"

"Nope. Figured it might be worth something to you. But I left a note, so don't think about killing me too."

At least he intended to leave a note.

"What do you want?"

He sounded afraid. At least he thought it was fear.

"Nothing for now, while we're locked up here. But when we get out, you and I need to have a little chat."

"Money, I suppose."

"You must have some, a professional like yourself."

"Someone's coming. We can talk later."

The killer charged up the backstairs as Thomas opened the door to the kitchen.

"Need any help with the wood?"

"Not for now. It's all good."

And it was going to be great for a long time with his little gold mine.

Chapter Eleven

P assing the door to the playroom, Anne saw Eloise rocking Hamish. Olivia played with her doll-house in one corner but ran to hug Anne when she came in. "Hello, Olivia. What have you been doing this morning? Lessons?"

"Not today. Eloise says it's a sad day and we don't have to do work."

"She's right. It is a sad day. I'm going to talk to Eloise for a little while."

"Okay."

Olivia scooted back to her corner, and Anne sat in another rocking chair, padded with a chintz-covered cushion. She leaned back and took a deep breath.

"Was it tough downstairs?"

"Yes, it was."

"Does Andrea think I killed Vanessa."

"Yes."

Eloise's eyes filled with tears. "She wants Hamish, and if she can say I'm a killer, she can take him from David."

Anne shook her head. "Don't you think she would have to prove that David is a killer, too. She's not rational, and the more she drinks, the less rational she becomes."

"So all David must do is fire me?"

Eloise voice dissolved in a sob. "He's not going to do that, Eloise. You take such care of the children."

"I love them."

"And David too, I think."

"For a long time. They will say that is why she is dead. Jealousy. She was une croqueuse de diamants."

"Gold-digger?"

Eloise leaned forward and nodded her head. "Yes."

"There are others with motives. But it takes a hating or frightened person to kill."

Then Anne remembered Colette. The Swiss woman killed on assignment and for revenge and almost killed her.

"I don't hate anyone," said Eloise.

A knock at the door brought Brad into the room. "Hi. Could I play with Hamish for a little while?"

At the word *play*, Hamish wiggled down from Eloise's knee and dumped his lego on the floor.

"I'll be going," said Anne. It was time she talked to Thomas.

Brad knelt down beside Hamish. The blue, yellow, and red interconnecting rectangles, oversized to help unsteady toddler fingers push them together, tumbled out of their wicker basket onto the carpet. Across the room, Olivia's unsmiling face stared at him. Why didn't the child like him? She never had. Eloise floated up from her chair. Nice legs, he thought, appreciating the view from his vantage point on the floor.

"If you stay here for a few minutes, I will shower, if there is any hot water," said Eloise.

"I don't think so."

"I've showered in cold water before."

"No running water at all, not for the taps, not for the toilets."

"What will we do?"

"Ask David."

The door crashed open, and Andrea pushed into the room, elbowing Eloise aside in her rush. "Did you get anything out of her?" she said when the door closed behind her.

"She's gone to talk to David about the water situation. What's the matter with you? Little pitchers have big ears, or did you not notice Olivia in the corner."

"What? Oh yes. Hello, Olivia."

"Can I go to the bathroom?" Olivia said.

"Where is it?"

"Over there."

She pointed to a door across the room.

"Away you go," said Brad. "But don't flush."

"Why?"

"Just don't."

"What are we going to do now. I want to leave here before someone kills us too."

"No one's going to kill us."

Brad helped Hamish place his train on the miniature track they had built. The little boy added blue plastic people to the yellow railway cars and plastic cows to the freight car. He woo-wooed his way around the track.

Andrea collapsed into the rocking chair. "What's going to happen to the children now that she's dead."

"More chance for us."

"Why do you say that? David will take the children and the little French sweetie, go back to Toronto, and leave us with nothing."

"Maybe. Or maybe whoever killed Vanessa isn't finished. I mean, why kill her? Why not him? He's the one controlling all the money. If he goes, the family will get Hamish for sure."

"Brad, you didn't—"

"Didn't what? What crazy idea to you have in your gin-soaked head now."

"I don't drink gin. It sounded like you wanted David dead."

"You want Hamish, don't you?"

"Not for me. For Trevor and Carmel."

"What? In the state she's in?"

"She'll be all right when she has a child to care for. Why does David, a single guy, want the kids anyway?"

"Maybe he's one of those—"

Horror crossed her face and her eyes popped, the whites scarlet with distended veins from the booze. God, what now?

"Brad, no. Oh, no. Do you really think so? We can't let him keep the children. We can't. What am I going to do?"

She lurched across the room and out the door.

That sure wound her up, thought Brad. When they left this godforsaken place they would start proceedings again.

In her room next door, Eloise flipped on the intercom that allowed her to hear the children when she wasn't with them. What was this? Appalled, she listened as Brad poured suggestions into Andrea's alcoholic brain. How could he do that? What should she do?

If she accused them of making up lies about David, they might suggest that she, too, was involved in whatever sick scheme they imagined David planned.

When Andrea left, she walked back to the playroom and sat down in the chair opposite Brad.

"You like these kids," he said.

"I love them very much."

"And what about Dave? You planning to take over from Vanessa there too."

"What do you mean "take over" and what do you mean "too". Vanessa had no interest in the children."

"Vanessa didn't like us," said Olivia from her corner.

"Of course she liked you. She was going to be your mother," Brad said.

"I have a mother, only she can't look after me right now."

Brad knitted his eyebrows and cast a quizzical glance at Eloise.

"Where?"

"Passed away."

The small voice piped up from the corner.

"Vanessa didn't want to be our mother, and she wanted to spank me. She would spank Hamish, too."

Brad frowned again at Eloise.

"What's the kid talking about?"

"Threats."

Eloise folded her arms and leaned back in the rocker. Why was he asking all these questions? It sounded as though he was accusing her of killing Vanessa. What could she do?"

Brad focussed on her from the other chair. He looked like a snake, she thought with his narrow eyes and the way he looked without blinking. She wished he would go.

"Hamish needs his nap."

"I thought he napped in the afternoon."

"He isn't sleeping well."

"Fine."

He stood up, brushed off his pants, and walked out of the room without speaking to Hamish, who whimpered at being left. Quel homme mauvais.

He had to be stopped before his poison affected everyone, especially his mother. What did she say? Something about what could she do. Andrea's brain was not normal. Perhaps she would do something mad. She would tell Anne and Thomas. They would know what to do.

Someone knocked at the door, her heart jumped, but she forced her self to answer calmly.

"Come in."

Beth opened the door to the nursery at Eloise's call to come in.

"Good morning. I wondered if I could spell you a little with the children, if you would like a break."

Eloise opened her eyes wide in surprise. Perhaps no one offered to help her much, Beth thought. She really was lovely. Why had David chosen Vanessa with this beautiful woman around all the time?

"I'd love to go downstairs for a half-hour or so. You are sure you don't mind?"

"I'm not experienced with children, although Kevin's sister has two sweet little girls that we mind sometimes."

"Hamish loves playing with his trains and likes someone with him on the floor, but Olivia likes to draw and paint at her table. Sometimes, I fear she is a bit neglected when people come to visit. Hamish is such a charming little boy that he gets all the attention."

"I love to draw too."

"I won't be long."

Beth walked over to Olivia.

"Olivia, my name is Beth, and I wondered if I could sit with you for a little while. Eloise says you like to draw and so do I. May I look at your work?

Olivia handed her a drawing of the people, a little more advanced than stick figures, with clothes and features.

"That is very good. Do you want to paint when you grow up?"

"No, I'm going to build houses. Beautiful houses with no yelling allowed."

"You don't like yelling?"

"No."

"Was someone yelling at you?"

Olivia nodded her head and took her purple crayon from the tray, added a dress to one figure, and replaced the crayon in its proper position on her tray.

"Do you want to talk about it?"

Olivia shook her head and went on colouring.

"When you are finished, would you like me to read to you. I'm a very good reader."

"Yes, please."

She pointed to a case against the furthest wall.

Half-an-hour later, both children were in Beth's lap on the rocking chair, sound asleep. Eloise opened the door and smiled.

"Thank you."

"They wanted the book read three times and promptly fell asleep."

"Bien sûr. David reads to them at bedtime."

Beth noted the touch of pink across Eloise's cheeks when she mentioned David. Like that, was it? Perhaps her brother and her mother would be defeated in their plans to take the children away. They should stay with this woman and David who loved them so much and had no substance abuse, like her mother or greed, like her brother. She would go to the court and say so if needed.

"May I come again?"

"Of course."

Eloise lifted Hamish and settled him in his crib. Olivia woke, Eloise tucked her blanket around her on the sofa, and the little girl slept again.

Beth left and opened the door of their room. Perhaps they should rethink the decision about children. Perhaps if they moved some-where other than Manhattan they could afford it.

She smoothed the fine wool sweater she wore, dusted off her black designer jeans, and crossed the room to wake Kevin.

Anne walked into their room to find Thomas stretched out on the perfectlymade bed, reading. His military service, she supposed, accounted for the precision. The drapes were open, but the windows revealed only swirling and gusting snow. The sweet scent of pine floated up from the crackling fire. Anne sat beside the simple red-brick fireplace and held her hands out to the flames.

"It's getting chillier by the minute in this house."

"The generator powered the pump at the outdoor furnace. No hot water either and the woodpile is going down, too."

She joined him on the bed, and he pulled the quilt around her.

"What do you think about David's request?" she said.

"At least we could search the room and take photos."

"Every time this happens and—why does it keep happening to us—we get sucked in further and further until one of us is hurt. Colette could have killed you or me or both of us last year."

"But she didn't. This is about preserving evidence, not investigating with it."

"What about supplies. Gloves?"

"There are disposable gloves in the workshop. They'll do, and I have my camera."

"The one on your phone? Is it still charged?"

"No, another small one with batteries."

"Well done, you."

He got out of bed and settled in the chair opposite her. Concern filled his eyes.

"Are you doing okay? No flashbacks or nightmares?"

"Not so far."

She reached over to touch his hand. She loved his strong hands with the long fingers that could be so gentle. He folded her hand into his.

"If people know we are poking around, someone, the killer might attack one of us."

"We'll stick together."

"Whom do you suspect?"

"Everyone else although some less than others. I can't see Eloise in a frenzy."

"She loves David and thinks Vanessa was a gold-digger, and she fears the loss of the children."

"Reason enough, but does she have it in her to kill like that? I don't think so."

"What about David?"

"No motive. Would you like something to drink? Tea?"

"Yes, let's go down, but what about Brad or Andrea?"

"Andrea, in a drunken frenzy, yes. Brad, no. Mike?"

"Why would he?"

Thomas offered her a hand up out of her chair, and they stood by the door for a moment.

"Trevor and Carmel?"

"They have enough trouble with her anorexia."

"After the tea, we can photograph the room. We may have to move the body to preserve it."

"The key?"

"In my pocket."

"We don't know enough about these people."

"Keep talking to them. That's what you do best."

"Talk?"

"Getting people to talk to you."

She laughed at that.

"An occupational skill."

They walked together down the hallway towards the stairs. Anne shook her head. They shouldn't involve themselves. Not again.

Chapter Twelve

When Anne and Thomas came down the back stairs into the kitchen, they found Mike and David at the table, shivering, their hands wrapped around steaming mugs,.

"Wood again?" Thomas said.

"Trying to thaw that goddamned generator but no luck. She's still dead," said Mike.

"The temperature's dropping outside, and the wood supply's going down trying to keep fires in all the rooms," said David.

"Perhaps everyone should spend the daytime in the living room or in here and only heat the children's playroom and bedroom," Anne said.

She busied herself at the stove. Food and water were not the problems; toilets and showers were.

"How would that go over with the others?"

"They can always gather some deadfall if they don't like it. Plenty in the bush," Mike said.

"Do you want help with that now?" Thomas asked.

"Not today."

Anne poured tea into cups, carried one to Thomas, and sat beside him across from David.

"What will we do about the toilets. I don't think I can melt enough water to flush them."

"There are emergency pots under each bed," said David.

"Thundermugs? Really?"

"Dad believed in being prepared. There's an outhouse attached to the woodshed. The men can go outside, and we can take the pots there to empty."

"Nice duty," Thomas said. "Whose?"

David grunted and lifted one side of his mouth in a grimace. "Each family takes care of its own.'

"You asked us to help with this," Anne said. "We would like to take photographs and search the room, in case we move her outside."

"Move her? I thought you opened the windows."

"We did, but it may not be cold enough, and we should preserve the body. In the shed perhaps, if we don't get power on again soon."

"I don't think you should meddle with the scene, and the cops will be pissed," said Mike.

David frowned again. "I want to make sure they have the evidence they need.'

Mike leaned forward and slapped the table. "So leave it alone and don't let these amateurs mess it up."

What had got into him? Why did he care one way or the other, Anne thought. His face was contorted with what? Anger, grief? She wondered what relationship he had with Vanessa.

"We won't disturb anything," Thomas said.

"All the same."

David closed his arms across his chest, and his jaw clenched. The skin over his cheekbones blanched. How curious Anne thought. Most people flush when they're angry. "Give it up, Mike. My house, my decision and on me."

"Have it your way but don't say I didn't warn you."

Mike swung out of his chair, grabbed his coat and boots, and slammed the door behind him. The others eyed each other. Thomas dark eyebrows lifted. Anne walked to the sink and leaned forward over the sink to catch a glimpse of Mike. Outside, he plodded away towards the woodshed, his arms hanging heavy at his side, his face to the ground. Grief, Anne thought. Not anger.

"What was that all about?" Anne asked.

"Who knows. You do what you have to do upstairs."

"We'll take pictures and have a quick look around. But that's all. No interrogating, no amateur interference," Anne said.

Brad knocked on Andrea's door and stalked in. Andrea perched in a yellow wing-back chair drawn up to the fire. The glass she held tumbled out of startled fingers, fell to the floor, and rolled beneath the bed. Her neglected grey hair fell in unkempt strings around her face, naked of makeup. She'd aged in two days.

"What did you do that for?" she said, her voice rising in a querulous whine.

"What?"

"Barge in here. You made me drop my glass."

"I told you to cut down on the drinking."

"It's my firsht, first one."

He drew the opposite chair closer to her.

"Sure, it is. Listen, as soon as we get out of here, we'll make a play for Hamish. That little minx is plotting something; I know she is."

"What minx? Carmel?"

"Carmel couldn't plot her way across a room. Eloise. She admitted that she loves the kids, so it's not just a job to her. We'll need to cast a lot of doubt on David. Can you cough up for a private detective?"

"Why?"

"To see if we can get anything on him. You remember I asked you why he wanted the kids."

"No, Brad. I don't believe it."

Her blue-veined hand with its paper-thin skin reached out to him. He pulled back from her touch. Old broad could keep her hands to herself. She covered her face for a moment, and he thought she sobbed, once. She uncovered her eyes, round with fear.

"Do you want Hamish or don't you?"

"Yes, yes. Get me my glass."

"And clean yourself up. No one would let you adopt a cat the way you look now."

Her head jolted back as though at a blow and tears filled her red-rimmed eyes.

"For chrissakes, Ma."

He reached under the bed for the glass and poured her a generous Scotch.

They'd get their hands on that money one way or the other, but right now he had to find out what everyone else was doing.

Thomas unlocked the door to Vanessa's room, and they stepped inside. The lock clicked behind them. Anne shivered from the cold that crept into her bones or was it something else, something that lingered in the room from the hate. Only hate fuelled those savage thrusts into Vanessa's body.

"Brr," said Anne. "Do you think we'll have to move her. It must be below zero Celsius in here."

"Not cold enough for many more days."

Anne tore her eyes away from the shrouded mass on the bed. The furniture in this room didn't follow the country pattern of the rest of the lodge. Anne thought they must be over the dining room from comparing the dimensions of the room. A white mantel decorated with acanthus leaves enclosed smooth black marble around the firebox of yellow brick. An ornate brass fender protected an Aubusson-style rug in black and cream from the embers.

Clothes from days before draped every surface: underwear in scarlet and black on one chair; silver shoes abandoned under the bed; elegant trousers in raw silk; a yellow evening dress she must have worn in the days before they arrived tossed on another chair.

Crusts of bread and the dregs of tea in a cup of fine porcelain, Worcester, she thought, remained on a tray on the bedside table. They needed to be preserved. Fine dust settled on the wooden surfaces.

An art-deco mahogany dressing table stood before a mirror framed in red lacquer. Crystal perfume bottles and expensive cosmetics lined up across the black marble top, in perfect order. A partially closed jewellery case in deep scarlet leather caught her eye. "Thomas, this case might have been searched. It's open."

He took photo after photo from every angle and squatted on the floor, shooting up into Vanessa's face. Anne shuddered but then focussed on Vanessa's head. Those strange ears, so like David's.

"Gloves?"

"Yes."

"Then go ahead and see if her jewellery is still there."

She lifted the lid and gasped at the trove of diamonds and rubies that filled the upper compartment. She assumed they were real and gifts from David. The edge of a paper peeked out from under the top tray. "Lots still here so I doubt anything is missing. Can you take a picture before I lift out the tray."

When Thomas was done, she inspected the paper below. A photocopy of a birth certificate. Vanessa Amanda Donland, mother, Emily Louise Donland. The name of the father had been written in by hand and read Cooper Thwaite. She turned it over. A letter from a genetics lab with DNA results. The individuals tested, it read, are half-siblings and share twenty-five percent of their DNA.

She staggered back and would have sat but remembered that she couldn't. Thomas took her arm. "Oh, my God."

"What is it?"

"You must photograph this."

He centred the camera on the document, clicked and then read it. "What kind of scam was she running?"

"What do we tell him?"

"Are you done? Let's go back to our room," said Anne.

She wanted to spend no more time in this freezing room, full of deceit and venom. Vanessa must have hated David to go to the extreme of bigamy and incest. But how could she? And how far did she take it? And did David find out? Was it he who rifled the jewellery box?

Before they left, she glanced in the closet. A tiny purple horse with a flowing pink mane lay abandoned at the back of the closer. "Olivia has been in here, in the closet, likely hiding. Should I—"

"Leave it in place."

He took a quick series of pictures of the closet. They left the room, and Thomas locked it behind them. "We have to talk," he said.

Chapter Thirteen

Eloise rapped on the doorframe by the stairs. Anne busied herself at the counter, filling the basket of the old-fashioned percolator with freshly ground coffee and water she melted from the snow Mike brought in. Thomas sat at the table set with mugs and milk for two. Both turned to her at her knock.

"May I come in, Anne?"

"Of course. You don't have to ask to come into the kitchen."

Eloise slipped into a chair across from Thomas. "I thought you might be talking."

"Let me get you a mug."

He took a porcelain mug, dotted with yellow daisies, from the cupboard and put it in front of Eloise.

"Merci. Do you have a minute to talk to me?"

Anne raised a quizzical eyebrow at her. How perceptive she was, Eloise thought. She knew how much she loved David before anyone else did.

"Both of us?" said Anne.

"Yes. I overheard something."

"Who?" said Anne.

"What?" said Thomas.

Eloise laughed, a charming tinkle that went up and down a scale but then the corners of her mouth drooped, and she squeezed her fingers together in front of her.

"Brad and Andrea. They were playing with the children when I slipped out to the bathroom. David wired the playroom so I can hear them from the bathroom and my room."

"What were they talking about?"

"Hamish, and getting him away from David, and wondering why David wanted the children. He suggested that David —David—"

"David what?" said Anne.

"David was one of those men."

"Do you mean predators," said Thomas.

"Oui, mais oui. That is what she meant. That's not true. It can't be true."

"We'll have to watch Brad," said Thomas.

"I think the mother is far more dangerous; she's so erratic. Folle."

"Crazy?"

"Oui, crazy with booze. I am afraid of what she will do now if she thinks David—"

"Bring the children down to play as much as you can. Call one of us if you need to leave them," said Thomas.

"Bien sûr. I will try."

She sipped the drink Anne poured for her and related Brad's exact words. "I think she ran away from him, but I'm not sure where she went. I'd better go back up to the children."

Andrea tossed the empty bottle of scotch in the trash and looked out the window at the falling snow, lighter now. She saw the outline of the dark pines around the field.

What should she do? What should she do? That man was going to hurt the baby. Her tears overflowed, and she sobbed.

No, she thought. No. She wouldn't let him do that to Hamish.

What had Brad meant? Was that what he said? She tried to remember, but all that came was fear for Hamish.

If the storm let up, she could take a snowmobile and escape. She was sure she could. There must be another property close by. Surely less snow was falling, and she could go now.

But how would she reach him? The little witch was always there. Eloise had to go to the bathroom sometime.

She crept down the hall to where the door to the playroom stood ajar. She waited.

Finally, she heard Eloise say, "I'm going to the bathroom, right here. You watch Hamish for me."

"I will," said Olivia.

"Promise. Don't sneak out."

"I won't."

Andrea heard the door to the bathroom open and close. Did she click the lock? She pushed into the room. Hamish played on the floor, and Olivia sat at her table. She rushed across the room, scooped up the little boy, ran out the door, and down the hall to the stairs. Behind her, Olivia screamed for Eloise. Hamish whimpered on her shoulder. She whispered, trying to sooth the little boy.

The kitchen was empty. Good. Andrea wrapped Hamish in a blanket, crammed her feet into her boots, and stepped outside the shed. The keys. Where were the keys for the snowmobiles? She remembered. On hooks by the kitchen door. Numbers marked in red. She took number seven. People shouted somewhere in the house, looking for her. Trying to stop her. Run, Run.

A path worn by the wood-gatherers led from the house to the shed. Beyond that, David kept the snowmobiles in an open-walled barn under covers. The covers. How heavy were they? Could she pull them off?

No footprints marred the snow beyond the woodshed. Andrea plunged forward into the snow; her feet slipped on the ice and she collapsed to her knees. Hamish screamed and yelled for Eloise. She hushed him, struggled to stand, and crashed to her knees again. The shouting came closer.

✻

Anne washed her hands and finished putting on a touch of blusher and mascara.

"Anne, Thomas, help."

Eloise. Anne jerked open the door, interrupting Eloise in mid-knock.

"Andrea's taken Hamish."

"Taken him where?"

What got into that drunken brain? And how much danger was the child?

"I don't know."

"She went downstairs," said Olivia, peeking out from behind Eloise.

Then she was taking him outside, into the storm.

"I'll find her. You and Olivia find Thomas or David and wait in the kitchen where it's warm."

Downstairs, a blast of freezing air met her. The kitchen door hung open. The wind rushed in and rattled the row of snowmobile keys, but number seven was missing. Did Andrea think she could escape with Hamish?

Anne grabbed a jacket, stuck her feet in someone's, a much bigger someone's, boots and tramped along the trail to the shed. The snow, heavier now, obscured the landscape beyond the building.

Andrea's struggling figure loomed, a dark shape ahead of her, and Hamish's cries, dampened by the storm, reached her.

How was she going to pull her up and keep Hamish safe? Behind her, someone called her name. Thomas?

The old woman struggled on the ice, still clutching a wailing Hamish, his pyjamas soaked and snow caking on his head and eyelashes.

"Andrea, give Hamish to me, and I'll help you up."

"No. I have to keep him safe."

"He's hurt. His chin is bleeding. Don't you see the blood?"

Anne reached for the baby and plucked him from Andrea's arms.

Andrea fell into the snow and lay there, her shoulders heaving. "He'll hurt him."

"He won't. That's nonsense."

"Brad—"

"Brad was winding you up."

Thomas reached them.

"Go back to the house with Hamish. You're both freezing. I'll look after her."

Anne passed David on his way to help Thomas. Their eyes met, and he nodded once, but raced on.

In the kitchen, Eloise stripped Hamish, towelled him off, and redressed him in the clothes she'd warmed by the fire. Anne dashed up to her room, grabbed her medical bag, and was cleaning the scrape on his chin when the two men returned with Andrea strung between them like a bag of heavy laundry.

"Put her near the stove," Anne said. "I'll check her ankles."

"She can't or won't walk," said Thomas.

Beth and Kevin came down the stairs with Olivia, who ran to David. He picked her up and cuddled her. Beth and Kevin pushed open the door to the living room and disappeared inside. Not concerned about her mother or too angry to talk to her?

Anne examined the ankles, testing for signs of a break. The Ottawa rules, she thought, remembering to check three points for pain that would indicate a broken bone.

"Nothing fractured, but she has a bad sprain. I'll wrap it for her."

David stood in front of the elderly woman, his feet planted wide, and his face contorted with fury. "Where did you think you were taking Hamish?"

"Away from you, you pervert."

David drew back and glanced at the others. "Does anyone know what she is talking about?"

"Brad suggested to her that you had evil designs on the children," Thomas said.

"What?"

"He wants his hands on the child and the money, I imagine," said Anne.

Andrea shifted in her chair and looked down at Anne, who wound a tensor bandage around her foot and ankle.

"What do you mean?" said Andrea.

"He wants you to have custody so he can access Hamish's trust."

"But, but."

At that moment, Brad and Trevor walked into the room. "What's going on?"

"Your mother tried to run away with Hamish on a snowmobile, but she fell and sprained her ankle. Apparently, you suggested danger to Hamish. If she had succeeded in leaving on a machine, they both would have died, and that would have been on you," Thomas said.

Brad's face lost all colour, and he fell into a chair. "I wanted her to proceed with a legal suit."

"Meanwhile telling her I was a pedophile, you louse."

David grabbed Brad's shirt collar and dragged him from the chair. It flipped backwards, crashing into the door behind. Thomas's hand gripped David's fist, before it slammed into Brad's face. "Put him down, Dave. You don't want to do this."

David threw Brad back against the table and stepped back. "You—"

Brad shook his head. "She took it that way. I didn't say that."

"I heard you," said Eloise.

"I'm, I'm sorry."

"You mean it'th, it's not true," said Andrea. "You made it up?"

"Now, Mom."

"No. I could have killed him. You always were a liar, from a child."

Brad stumbled away from the table and through the swinging doors to the living room, followed by Mike and Trevor.

"Always a liar," said Andrea, her speech slowing and her eyelids drooping.

But was he also a killer, Anne wondered.

❄

Frantic voices in the hallway drew Beth out of her room. Anne and Eloise rushed down the back stairs but Olivia, abandoned, stood at the door of the nursery.

"Olivia, come here and tell me what's wrong."

Olivia's eyes filled with tears, and she hugged Beth's legs. "Eloise said to look after Hamish, but that lady came and took him away."

"Which lady?"

Olivia knuckled her eyes. "Mrs. Barr—I don't know."

"Barrington?"

"Yes."

Beth picked up the child and called Kevin. "Kevin, come downstairs. Mom did something really stupid this time."

She carried Olivia to the stairs, but the child squirmed until she put her down. Olivia's hand crept into hers. Kevin reached them and asked what had happened.

"She took Hamish," Olivia said.

"What's that, sweetheart?"

"She came into our room, and picked him up, and ran away."

"Let's go down and help," Beth said.

Kevin followed them down the stairs into the kitchen, in time to see Anne and Hamish come back. When Thomas and David returned with Andrea, Beth walked away into the living room. Kevin followed her, leaving Olivia clinging to David.

"Beth?" said Kevin.

Beth turned dry, angry eyes to him. "She has to go somewhere to dry out. We can't go on with her doing increasingly dangerous things."

He folded his arms around her but she shrugged away.

"After we're out of here, we'll make a plan."

"What will we do if she won't—"

"Later."

He gathered her into his arms, and she clung to him, reassured by the strength and common sense that flowed into her from his embrace.

By lunchtime, Anne had searched the freezer and found enough food for several meals. The cook must be a baker, she thought, counting the loaves of bread, cakes, cookies and pies stacked on one side and on the other, packages of simple-to-cook meats, like steaks and chops and casseroles of chicken and ground beef.

The bread thawed quickly in the warming oven of the wood stove. The eggs, perishable and a health risk if left too long out of the fridge, she carried to the cold room. She made egg salad and put together sandwiches. Those and pickles and spiced olives would do for lunch. She set the table and rang the dinner bell.

Thomas burst through the swinging doors. "Are you all right?"

"Lunchtime."

He wrapped his arms around her. "You do scare me."

Before he said more, others arrived, and they sat, mostly in silence. Carmel ate a corner of a sandwich and drank water.

Mike wolfed down three sandwiches, three cups of coffee and two generous slices of cake. Eloise chattered away as she fed the children, but the others sat in silence.

Anne carried a tray of sandwiches and coffee over to Brad and Andrea, who huddled near the stove. Andrea's bony fingers encircled her wrist, like a snare of twigs. Why so bony when the rest of her was well-padded? Anne pried her arm loose. "What is it?"

"What are you going to do with me?" Andrea asked, her voice trembling and slurring her words.

"I wrapped your ankle."

"No, what will you tell the police?"

"We'll have to tell them everything that happened this weekend, but that will include why you thought you had to rescue Hamish. I don't think anything will happen to you."

Andrea's face crumpled into the easy tears of the drunk, and she clutched at Anne. Anne moved away from the grasping hand.

"Thank you, thank you."

"It's just the truth, Andrea."

Back at the table, David scowled into his lunch and rounded his hands into fists. "She shouldn't get off that easily."

Eloise patted his hand. "She isn't responsible, David."

David looked into the upturned face and smiled. He beams, Anne thought, as though he'd never seen her before. And maybe he hadn't. At least not that way.

Chapter Fourteen

After lunch, Anne and Thomas slipped away to their room.

"We have to talk," he said.

"About the situation here or about us?"

"Eventually about us, but you said you would decide by the time we left. Are you closer?"

He stood at the window, one arm raised to hold the frame, his back stiff. What could she say? She didn't want to lose him, but she still wasn't sure about committing to marriage. "All I can think about is this trouble and if anyone else is in danger."

"Tomorrow is the day we should be leaving, will you be certain by then?"

"I hope so. I hope we can find out who killed Vanessa and move on to our problems."

Her voice broke. Thomas left the window and sat beside her on the bed. "We're together whatever you decide."

He put his arms around her, and she snuggled against his chest. Did he mean that she wondered? He said it now, but for the future?

A staccato knock at the door interrupted her thoughts.

"Who is it?" Thomas asked.

"David."

Thomas stood back from the door and opened it with his left

hand. Always so careful, she thought. The CIA training stayed with him, always. The door swung open, David walked in, and Thomas closed the door behind him.

David swung back, his hands curled into fists, but he relaxed when he saw Thomas. He cleared his throat.

"Sorry to bother you, but I wondered if you had found anything in Vanessa's room. Are you any closer to figuring out what went on here?"

"You'd better sit down," Thomas said.

David, his face furrowed and panic in his eyes, found the chair behind him, and sank into it. He leaned forward, peering into Thomas's face and glanced at Anne, for reassurance, she thought. She couldn't smile; couldn't give him that.

"What is it?"

Thomas handed him the birth certificate and DNA results. When he finished reading, he frowned and shook his head. Like a confused dog, Anne thought. Not sure where to turn. "What does this mean? Who wrote Dad's name on this? Who tested my DNA?"

"You don't recognize the handwriting? We wondered if it was Vanessa's," said Anne.

"It looks like hers, but why—"

"Either it's true, and she was your half-sister, or she was planning a scam or blackmail after you went through a marriage ceremony with her, or both," Thomas said.

"I think Vanessa was your half-sister," said Anne. "You and she and Hamish share those same family ears your father had. She was very interested in your family genealogy and wanted me to investigate for her."

His swift reaction suggested he hadn't known, that his response was genuine. "My sister."

David bolted into the bathroom, leaving the door open behind him. Sounds of retching reached them and then of the water running. Not too hard to fake, but genuine, she thought.

When he came back, his face pale and sweat beading on his forehead, he said, "I'm sorry. You know we—"

"Yes."

He moaned and hid his face in his hands. An ancient taboo broken, Anne thought. Something no one thinks about but almost all obey. Hardwired into humans, she supposed.

"How could she? How could she?"

"She must have wanted money and perhaps to punish you for being acknowledged when she wasn't," said Anne.

"Dad would've acknowledged her if he'd known she existed. Why would he exclude one child?"

His eyes swung between Anne and Thomas, searching.

"Who knows why she chose this way?" Thomas said. "But she did, and you see that it gives you a motive for killing her."

"But I didn't know. I didn't know."

He collapsed back into the chair and sobbed, holding his head in his hands, rocking.

Anne and Thomas waited, sitting side by side on the bed. Either he is a consummate actor or he had no idea, she thought.

David raised his face, rubbed away the tears, and stuck out his jaw. "I didn't kill her and I want you to find out who did. Was there anything else in the room?"

"No," said Thomas.

He didn't want her to mention Olivia's toy, Anne thought. Not to anyone.

After a time, David stood up and left without a word.

"Hard to take," Thomas said.

"Genuine, I think."

"Yes. We'd better go down to see what's happening with everyone else."

Anne and Thomas came into the kitchen in time to hear Trevor ask Mike where the dogs were. Andrea and Brad sat together at one end of the pine table, Trevor and Mike at the other. At the counter beside the sink, Eloise spooned bright-orange toddler food into a Bunnykins bowl.

"Outside, I think," said Mike. "They came out with me when I went for wood."

"Has anyone fed them today?"

Eloise looked around from feeding Hamish. "Bien sûr," said Eloise. "I feed them when I get the breakfast for the children."

Trevor crossed over to the back door and whistled. The two dogs emerged from the falling snow, covered in white, their tails down. Trevor grabbed the dog towels from their hooks by the door and dried first Andy, the poodle, and then Max.

The pungent odour of wet dog soon mingled with the cooking smells. A scent that always made her happy, Anne thought, that brought back home and the small hound she loved so much when she was young.

David clattered down the stairs, rubbed Andy's head and sat at the table with the others. Calmer, Anne thought. He was resilient; he'd cope.

"Why did you bring them in here, Trevor? They stink," said Brad.

"Don't you start. And the dogs smell clean from the snow to me. Where did you want them to go, back out into the storm?" said David, rubbing the poodle's ears.

"I'll take them up with me. There is a fire in the playroom," said Eloise.

She gathered up the children and called the dogs who climbed the stairs with her, Andy ahead and Max plodding behind.

"A nice woman," said Trevor.

"What do you mean nice? That little witch wants the children," said Andrea. "Who knows what she would do to get them?"

"What are you talking about?" said David. "She's paid to look after them. Perhaps you should take your mother into the living room, Brad."

"Cold in there."

"So, build a fire."

Brad helped Andrea up and dragged her with him through the swinging doors.

David and Mike bundled into their clothes and went back out to bring in more wood. Trevor left, saying he wanted to check on Carmel.

"Getting restless," said Thomas.

"Me, or the natives?"

"The natives. And I don't like it."

"You think the killer's not finished?"

"Yes."

Chapter Fifteen

B rad settled Andrea onto the sofa near the fireplace. The cold of the room swallowed most of the heat from the flames, but enough reached them to warm them. Andrea shivered and hugged her arms to her body. She was old, he thought. When did she become so old?

"I want a glass of brandy. "I've got a chill."

"I'm sure. What were you thinking, trying to run away?"

He poured two fingers of amber cognac into a snifter and carried it back to her.

"I had to save him from David. You said—"

"I didn't. All I said was that we didn't know why he wanted the kids. Now you've done it. We can never adopt Hamish after you endangered him. And while you're still drinking."

"There's been a murder. I'm frightened, Brad. Who did it? Did you?"

He jerked back from her and swore. "Now what's got into your gin-soaked brain? No, I didn't kill her. Why would I do that?"

"I don't drink gin. To take Hamish. Maybe without her, the courts won't—"

"You are nuts. When we're out of here, you're going to Homewood."

"Homewood?"

"A place to dry out."

"You can't put me away."

Her voice rose into a scream, and the kitchen door swung open.

"What's going on?" said Thomas.

"Nothing," said Brad. "She's a little upset."

Thomas returned to the kitchen.

"Who is he?" said Andrea. "Why is he in charge?"

"Busybodies, the pair of them," said Brad. "I won't put up with them investigating us."

"Why would—"

"Because of what you just did."

Andrea sank back against the cushions. Her face, usually pale, flamed scarlet and she shook.

"What's the matter?"

"I don't feel well."

"Going to be sick?"

"No, like I have a fever and—

A coughing spasm interrupted her speech. She leaned forward, her face purpled, and she clutched at Brad's hand. Her blue-tinged fingernails dug into his palm, and he shook her off.

"I need the doctor."

"Anne?"

"Yes."

"I'll take you upstairs and talk to her."

Eloise sorted the children's clothes into piles of clean and dirty. The clean piles got smaller every day, she thought. When would they ever go back home? She and the children and David lived in a rambling old house in Toronto's Rosedale neighbourhood, with an expansive garden for the children to play in and central heating. It was home to her, but should she stay? She had planned to hand in her notice when David married Vanessa, but now? Hamish stirred in his crib but lay quietly. Across the room, Olivia sniffed and wiped her hand across her nose.

"Olivia, use a tissue."

"My nose is dripping too fast."

"Viens-ci."

Olivia trod over to her, trailing her pink security blanket behind her. Eloise touched her forehead. No fever. She helped the little girl blow her nose and crossed to the crib to check on Hamish.

He lay on his back watching the mobile of farm animals rotate above him. Was he breathing too quickly? A coughing spasm racked his body and he struggled to sit up. She reached for him and held him against her. This one had a fever. She found her thermometer in the children's bathroom, inserted it in his ear. Thirty-nine degrees Celsius. Too high.

She said to Olivia, "Go find Doctor McPhail for me."

"Who?"

"Anne. Go find Anne. Hamish is sick."

Olivia dashed down the stairs to the kitchen and wrapped her arms around Anne's legs. Anne patted her hair while the little girl gasped out her message.

"Anne, Anne. Eloise says to come right away. Hamish is sick. His face is all red, and he is breathing like the dogs."

"I'm coming. Thomas, tell David when he comes in. What do you mean, breathing like the dogs?"

Olivia opened her mouth and took rapid short breathes.

"Panting."

Upstairs, she told Olivia to go back. "Tell Eloise I'm coming. I'm going for my bag."

In moments, she was kneeling beside the rocking chair. "Did you give him anything for fever?"

"Not yet."

Anne took a bottle of children's Advil, poured a dose and fed it to Hamish. She listened to his chest. The sibilant wheeze and rapid breathing told her he likely had bronchiolitis or respiratory syncytial virus. Or worse, influenza. And she had no resources here if he should worsen. "Is he fully immunized?"

"Yes."

"What about the flu shot?"

"Next week."

"I have a Ventolin puffer. Do you know how to use them?"

"Yes but he has his own and a mask. He's asthmatic."

"Okay. Give him two puffs now and then one puff as needed, up to every hour."

"Does he need an antibiotic? Does he have pneumonia?"

Eloise smoothed the child's hair, her eyes filled with worry. "No to both."

David rushed into the room and knelt beside the rocking chair. "What's wrong with him? Why didn't you call me, Eloise?"

He held one chubby hand in his long fingers. The child's breathing eased, and he struggled to take off the mask.

"A little while longer, Hamish. We need to keep the mask on till the medicine's all gone. He was fine when I put him down for his nap. He woke up with this."

"That's the way it starts," said Anne. "This virus hits fast, but we'll get ahead of it."

David sank into a chair, Olivia climbed into his lap and patted his face. "Don't worry, Uncle David. Eloise will look after us."

He looked at Eloise and managed a smile. Her lovely mouth curled upwards in response.

Anne gathered up her bag and left, closing the door behind her. Thomas met her in the hallway. "Everything okay?"

"Hamish has bronchiolitis."

"You're needed to see Andrea. She's pretty bad."

Brad settled his mother in her room, ignored her pleas for him to stay with her and slammed the connecting door to his single room. Worst room in the house, he thought. The little witch had her own and a private bath while he had to share with his mother. What man wants to share a bathroom with his mother? He stoked the fire and poured himself a scotch from the bottle he'd liberated from the dining room. David wouldn't miss it. His father left him a piss-potful of money but his? Not so much.

He answered a knock at the door with a snarled *who is it?*

"Beth."

"What the hell do you want?"

"We have to talk."

"We've nothing to say to each other."

"Open the door, Brad."

He turned the knob and his back and stalked across the room to where a pot-bellied stove let off a little heat into the room. "What?"

Beth settled herself into the one comfortable chair, leaving him with the straight-backed oak one at the desk. "Mom."

"What about her?"

"She's getting worse with the drinking."

"She's under a pile of stress here."

Beth shook her head. "She and the child could have died out there. She has no judgement, no sense when she's drinking, and she's always drinking. And you, filling her head with lies. All because—"

Her upper lip rose in disgust.

"All because?"

"Greed. You want to control Hamish's trust. We know it, David knows it, and it's not going to happen."

"Carmel—"

"You don't care about Carmel or the kids, or Mom for that matter."

He took a step towards her, his fists curled at his side.

"Don't even think about it. Kevin would take you apart."

Her eyes swept over him. God, she had cold eyes. He'd never noticed.

"Did you kill her?"

"Kill who? Vanessa? Are you nuts? Why would I—"

"Easier to make a claim for Hamish."

What was she thinking? What the hell? Who had she said that to?

"Beth, don't say stuff like that to those two "investigators". Of course, I didn't kill her. I couldn't kill anybody."

"Did Mom?"

"What's the matter with you? You know us. We're not killers. I made a stupid mistake and then Mom did."

She nodded. "Then what are we going to do about Mom and the drinking? She needs to dry out. Can you arrange that when we get out of here?"

"Perhaps."

"She's going to kill herself or someone else if you don't."

She stood, stared down at him for a moment, and stalked out the door.

Christ. Did the others suspect him? What was he going to do?

Chapter Sixteen

Trevor found Carmel in the bathroom attached to their bedroom. She stood naked, pinching the loose skin on her abdomen. "It's worse, Trevor. It's worse. See how much fat there is."

"No, sweetheart. No. Come away from the mirror. You have no fat. That's skin. Just skin."

"They'll never let us adopt Hamish if I'm fat. You know that. The social workers hate fat people."

"They don't. They can't discriminate like that, and you're not fat. You're too thin, and as long as you are dieting, those workers won't give us a baby, any baby."

He'd never said that to her. The psychiatrist said not to confront her, that they would do it. What the hell. They weren't here, trapped with two crazy women. But Carmel wouldn't be crazy if she had Hamish to care for. He knew she would be back to her old self then.

"They don't want me to diet?"

"No, they don't. Will you try to eat? Come and lie down for a little while."

She let him take her hand and lead her back to the bed. He tucked a quilt around her and piled two blankets on top. Cold ashes filled the fireplace. "I'm going to get some more wood. You sleep, and I'll bring you something to eat after."

"Yes, after."

Her words slurred, and she drifted off.

The only way to help was to adopt Hamish. The only way. What was he going to do?

Anne rushed along the hallway to Andrea's bedside. "How long have you been sick," she asked.

"Just an hour or so. I thought I had a chill from being outside."

Anne counted her respirations at eighteen breaths a minute. High for an adult. Her temperature sat at thirty-nine degrees Celsius. Her mute stare, from weepy blue eyes surrounded by pale flesh, pleaded for help.

"Help me sit her up."

She listened to the ageing heart and to the shallow breaths, punctuated by sibilant wheezes and the underneath rattle of fluid bubbling through air. She tucked an extra pillow at Andrea's back and lowered her. Andrea's face paled with the effort, and she closed her eyes.

"Andrea, you have pneumonia. Have you been diagnosed with chronic lung disease?"

Her eyelids opened, and she nodded.

"Do you use puffers?"

Andrea struggled to force the words out between gasps.

"Medicine chest."

In the bathroom, Anne found a bronchodilator and inhaled steroid and took them back to the bedside. From her bag, she took out a vial of medication.

"Do you have allergies to any antibiotic?"

She shook her head.

"I'll give you this in your bottom," Anne said, drawing up the liquid into a syringe.

Andrea recoiled back into her and cast a frantic glance at Brad.

"Find Eloise for me," Anne said, "And stay outside for a few minutes."

Eloise helped her give Andrea a shot of antibiotic and administer the puffers. After, Eloise wiped down Andrea's face and changed her nightgown. Andrea patted her hand. "Good girl. Thank you."

When her patient's breathing eased, Anne talked to Brad in the hall. "You stay with her for a few hours and call me if she seems worse in between my visits."

"Eloise—"

"No, Hamish is also ill, and Eloise must stay with him. I'll come by every hour but call me if there is any change."

"I will. Foolish old woman. This happened because she went outside."

"That didn't help, but she was afraid, and that's on you. Watch her."

Brad's pale face with its bulbous nose crumpled and he cried.

"Stop that. Your mother needs you. Go back in and try to be cheerful in front of her."

He passed his hand across his eyes, straightened, and walked back into his mother's room.

Chapter Seventeen

Mike confronted the killer standing in the bow window at one end of the long living room. Outside, the wind howled, and the pines at the edge of the lawn bowed towards the house. The wind direction had shifted again, Mike thought. Would the storm never end? Meanwhile, time to establish the rules with this guy.

"You know that I'm going to want some money."

"Don't have any here," the killer said.

"Why not?"

"Why would I bring money to a friend's place for a weekend. Free food, free booze, free toys. A wedding, I thought. No need for cash. David's rich as hell."

"Why did you try to kill him?"

"Who says I did?"

"You killed Vanessa."

"Try and prove it."

"So that's your game."

"We'll see what the cops have to say to your so-called evidence."

"You thought you hid your clothes, but you didn't, and now your shirt and your ass are mine."

The killer stalked down the room and through the door to the kitchen, his back stiff.

That went okay, thought Mike. The guy was scared but not too scared.

Chapter Eighteen

In the kitchen, Anne poured boiling water into the fat brown teapot and set her phone's timer for four minutes. Thomas placed cups and a package of ginger cookies on the table.

"A few minutes of peace. Can we talk?"

"About us? Not yet, Thomas. We have so much else. I'm worried about Andrea. She's older, and she's an alcoholic. That may mean her immune system is compromised. She got ill so quickly."

"So did Hamish."

"That's normal for his age, and he's not too bad. I only hope he doesn't have influenza A or B and that he has enough left in his puffers. Is there any other way we can send a message out of here? Could someone take a snowmobile?"

"Too much risk, I think. Snow's heavy and there's a thick layer of ice underneath it. A machine would get stuck or go across water without knowing it. The ice is not deep enough in the creeks and rivers to hold it up."

Anne passed a weary hand across her eyes.

"You've not been sleeping well. Have I put too much pressure on you?"

He reached for her hand across the table. How loving he is, she thought. And how foolish she was. She opened her mouth to speak when Trevor crashed through the door to the kitchen.

"What's up?" said Thomas.

Trevor leaned on the table. "Between my wife and all this other drama and a murder, how can you ask what's up? Can you visit Carmel?" he said, turning to Anne.

"Why?"

"She can't or won't leave her bed. I...it might be my fault. I told her they wouldn't let us adopt a baby as long as she was not eating."

"What did her psychiatrist advise?"

"That I shouldn't challenge her. But nothing is working. Nothing."

Anne's gaze met Thomas's. "I'll come up."

In Carmel's room, thick green drapes blocked the faint winter light, leaving a pool of yellow splashing over the bedside table from a frivolous French lamp. Carmel lay flat on her back, her eyes focussed on the ceiling. Restless fingers plucked at the bedspread. Anne opened the drapes and raised the window, releasing a rush of fresh winter air into the room.

Carmel's querulous voice reached her. "Why did you do that?"

"The air was stale and lying in the dark does you no good."

"Who—"

"Anne. Trevor asked me to come to you—"

"Don't you think you should keep her calm?" Trevor asked.

"I think you should wait outside."

"But—"

"She needs privacy to speak to a doctor."

"I always—"

"Not this time."

He hesitated but left, and Anne drew a chair up to the bed. "Do you want me to help you, Carmel?"

Carmel's face, filled with despair and something else—anger, perhaps—swung towards her. Her sunken eyes, ringed with dark circles, flashed with a sudden brilliance but faded into despair. "Can you find me a baby? No, I thought so. Doctors never help."

"You can have your own baby if you recover from this anorexia."

"I'm too fat. That's why I can't get pregnant."

The disordered thinking of those who suffered from this awful illness appalled Anne. How could she reach Carmel and help her? "That's what you think, but I imagine your gynaecologist said the opposite."

"Maybe."

"Trevor wanted to stay here. Why?"

"He loves me and wants the best for me."

Her voice said the words as though repeating a lesson.

"He likes to choose what you do?"

"That's what people do when they love you. My parents were the same."

"Are you an only child?"

"Yes."

"Do you think Trevor and your parents are to blame for your not eating."

Carmel's eyes reddened and her face flushed. "Of course not. I'm too fat, so I diet. If I stop, I'll become a monster."

"Has your psychiatrist told you that your thoughts are disordered, incorrect?"

Carmel's voice faltered. "They tried to make me think their thoughts. Like you."

"No, I don't want to make you to think my thoughts. I want you to think, though. Do about want to die?"

The emaciated face, with its haunted eyes, rolled towards her and away. "Sometimes."

But she didn't have to reach her, Anne thought. All she had to do was keep her alive until rescue came. "Today?"

She stared back at the ceiling or nothing. "Not today. Trevor says we can adopt Hamish if I eat. Is that true?"

"I don't know, but I think you need to be healthy. Can I take your pulse?"

"Yes. You people always want to take my pulse or my temperature. I'm not sick."

Anne counted a slow pulse of thirty-eight beats. Carmel's breath, with its odour of nail polish remover, a bad sign, reached Anne as she leaned towards her. "Yes, you are. We call your illness an eating disorder—Anorexia Nervosa—and you need careful treatment."

"Are you going to treat me? Everyone always does."

"No, I'm not. But I want you to stay alive long enough for us all to escape this place so someone who knows how can help you."

"I'm not going to kill myself."

"You may not intend to, but you are in danger. You must drink something and eat a little. Will you do that today?"

"Water."

"No, tea with milk. Will you do that? And eat a cracker."

"Yes, just one cracker."

Anne opened the door and Trevor stumbled into the room. "I'm going to bring Carmel some tea. Please sit with her without conversation but close the window first."

"I have—"

"No. She's had enough conversation for now."

The flames in the wood stove flickered in the grey ashes. Anne bundled in some newspaper and kindling and set the paper alight. In moments the kindling caught and she added a split log to the box. It must have gone out moments before, she thought. The water in the reservoir was still hot. She filled a kettle and waited, watching the snow fill up the window from the sill below. Beyond, two dark figures, laden with wood, ploughed through the fallen snow to the back door. Once inside, after they dumped the split logs beside the stove, they kicked off their boots and hung their parkas on the hooks.

"How's the wood supply?"

"Enough for a day or so," Thomas said. "I think we should cut back where we can."

"We need fires in Andrea and the children's room. I'm also worried about Carmel. Her pulse is dangerously low, and she needs to be kept warm. I've convinced her to drink some tea and eat a cracker."

Mike brushed his hands off over the wood box. "So long as the stove keeps going, I figure the rest of us will be all right."

"We walked along the lane towards the road," Thomas said.

A note in his voice brought Anne's attention to him. "What?"

"A power line down across the road. When the power comes back on, it will be live for sure, if not now. It will need repair before we have power again."

"So no leaving on snowmobiles?"

"When the snow lets up, I can go through the bush," said Mike, "but the way she's coming down, even I'd lose my way for sure."

Later, Anne carried tea to Carmel—a porcelain mug decorated with pink roses, a solitary cracker on the plate beside it. She knocked, opened the door, and strode into the murky room. Drapes drawn again. She put down the tea, jerked open the curtains, and raised the blinds.

"Too bright," said Carmel, throwing her arm over her eyes.

Who closed these for her? She told Trevor the girl needed light and air. Carmel lay back, hiding her face, her body rigid.

"Gloom isn't good for you. Sit up now and sip your tea."

Her voice sounded harsh, not firm as she intended.

"Did you put milk in it?"

"Yes."

"Too many—"

"No. We talked about this. You must drink, or you will become even sicker than you already are."

Hopeless, Anne thought. But she had to try.

Carmel struggled to sit but fell back, exhausted. The skin of her face blanched where it pulled taut over her knife-sharp cheekbones, and purple blotches stained the crescents under her sunken eyes. Anne put her arm around her and helped her. Bones, she thought. Just bones. After Carmel took a few sips, Anne handed her a cracker. A grimace passed over Carmel's face. "No."

"Yes. I have no other way to help you. Eat a little of it."

By the time Anne left, twenty minutes later, Carmel had eaten half the cracker, and nothing remained in her cup. A start, Anne thought, but only that.

Chapter Nineteen

Anne set the table and rang the dinner bell outside the door of the kitchen. Thomas laughed. "Try not to take it out on the bell, Anne."

"If they're hungry, I'll bet they'll all come down. Why doesn't anyone help? Eloise is the only one with anything to do, and she helps in here when she can."

David pushed open the door from the outside, his arms laden with wood. Behind him, Mike, with a similar burden, stamped the snow off his feet before he dumped his firewood beside the stove.

"Thanks, Anne," David said. "I should have been in here to help you."

"You had other work to do, you and Mike. I can't cook without wood. And that's something I never thought I'd have to say."

She opened the door to the oven and tested the sausage and pasta casserole with a red digital thermometer. "We're lucky there's so much food prepared ahead."

She drew on a pair of oven mitts, took out the dish, and put it on the stove-top.

"Will the children eat that?" David asked.

"Yes, it's kid-friendly food."

"I'll call them and Eloise," he said and bounded up the stairs.

Moments later, little feet raced down. David lifted Olivia into her booster seat, and Eloise strapped Hamish into his high-chair. Andrea and Brad followed them down. Andrea immediately went to Hamish and tried to lift him up. Hamish yelled.

"Andrea, he's strapped in. Leave him to eat his dinner."

"I can hold—"

"No. He has a routine. Sit down, yourself," said Eloise.

"I won't be ordered about by the likes of you."

"Sit down, Mom," said Brad.

Andrea grumbled to herself and poured the wine that appeared at her elbow.

Who put that on the table, Anne wondered, placing water glasses in front of the other plates.

"Is the milk still okay?" Eloise asked.

"Yes," said Anne. "I added some ice to a container in the fridge, and the temp is okay so far."

"Why do you know so much about coping with this stuff?" asked Andrea.

"I've been through it twice before."

"What did you do upstairs?" Mike said to Thomas.

"What do you mean?" said Brad.

"They "investigated" in Vanessa's room, even though we all agreed to lock it up and wait for the cops."

"Who investigated?"

"Anne and Thomas. They took—"

"Hold it," said David. "I asked them to take photos in case we had to move Vanessa's body outside.

"Why would you move it?" said Andrea.

Brad whispered in her ear, she blanched, and swallowed more wine.

"What did you take from Vanessa's room? She had expensive jewellery," Andrea said.

"And I'm sure that when David checks, he will see that it is all there. Be careful about your accusations."

Andrea settled back into her chair and looked at Thomas with frightened eyes. She was never sober, Anne thought and never entirely accountable.

"For heaven's sake, go easy on the wine, Mom," said Beth from the corner of the table furthest from Andrea.

"Leave Mom alone. Like you care?" said Brad.

"And you care so much you put wine at her elbow," said Kevin.

"I didn't do—"

"Yes, you did. I saw you."

"Would anyone like to go into the living room?" Anne said after they wolfed down the casserole and biscuits.

"I'll help with the cleaning-up if David takes the children," said Eloise.

The others left.

"That was unpleasant," said Eloise.

"Yes and the longer we're stuck here, the worse it's going to get."

The fire cast a cheerful glow over the circle of sofa and chairs. A peaceful family scene, Thomas thought, with David playing with the children. David's face lit up with a grin when Eloise came back into the living room. Thomas wondered how long David had loved Eloise and what he would have done to escape the wedding. Or had he not known. Some men were like that. He, on the other hand, knew what or rather who he wanted and had for all the time he'd known her. They just had to survive this weekend.

"Come, Olivia," Eloise said. "It's quiet-time."

The little girl stuck out her lower lip and knitted her eyebrows together. Stubborn, Thomas thought, but he suspected David and Eloise could handle her. "I want to stay with Uncle David."

"Grown-ups need quiet-time, too."

Olivia turned to David and used her most wheedling tone. "Uncle David?"

"Eloise decides, Olivia."

He lifted her, gave her a kiss, and put her down next to Eloise.

Eloise lifted Hamish into her arms, took Olivia's reluctant hand, and climbed the stairs.

She was good with the children, Thomas thought. David could do worse and almost did.

Anne brought in a tray of coffee and Trevor helped her hand the mugs around. She looked tired, Thomas thought. Worn down with the worry and the work. What else could he do to get her out of here?

"I'm going to check on Carmel," Trevor said. "I'll be back down."

Thomas glanced at his host, leaning back in one of the club chairs with his eyes closed. A faint snore fluttered across the room.

"How can he sleep," Brad said, "with Vanessa dead and all of us cooped up here with a killer? Why isn't he trying to find a way to reach the outside."

Across the room, David stirred but didn't waken.

"Up at first light to cut wood," Mike said.

"And who are you, anyway. Nobody knows you. Maybe you killed her."

"Who knows you? You're only here because Dave invited Hamish's grandmother, and you tagged along."

Thomas listened to the voices, shouting now, but watched David. No response. He heaved himself out of the soft chair and strode over to David, calling his name. He shook him and then pinched a muscle. Nothing.

He bolted to the kitchen door. Anne wasn't there. He raced up the stairs.

Anne stood at the window of their room for a few moments. The wind howled in the chimney and, across the lawn, the old pines nodded their fragile, ice-laden heads. And still, the snow fell. She turned away and picked up her book. Louise Penny's latest.

She looked up when the door swung open and was on her feet

before Thomas spoke. "Quick, something's wrong with David. I can't rouse him."

"I'll bring my bag."

Downstairs, she raced across the room, knelt by David's chair, and felt for a pulse in his neck. There. Slow but there. His breaths slipped out at long intervals. She checked his pupils. Pinpoint. Would he have taken narcotics or was someone trying to kill him too?

She glanced up at Thomas when he squatted beside her. "Opioids."

He opened her bag for her and she grabbed a package of auto-injectors and stabbed one into David's arm. After an agonizing few minutes, not long, although it seemed as though an hour passed, he moaned.

"David."

"Hmm."

"Open your eyes."

His eyelids fluttered and rose. His pupils were mid-point. "What?"

"Did you take something? Pills or a needle."

"What?"

"You have opioid in your system. Did you take something?"

"No."

She rolled up the sleeves of his blue cotton shirt. No marks of any kind. "Let's take him upstairs. I must stay with him."

"We have to stay with him. Help me, Mike."

The two men supported David to the stairs and half-carried him to his room.

"Walk him around for a bit, if you can," said Anne, coming in behind them.

"He can't."

Once he was on the bed, Anne retook his pulse and blood pressure and noted the size of his pupils. Thomas brought her a notepad from David's desk, and she charted the time and her findings.

"Will he need more?"

"Likely. That depends on the dose of opioid."

"Did you know?" Mike said.

"Know what?"

"That he was an addict."

Anne gazed up at him and shook her head.

"He isn't. Someone tried to kill him."

Chapter Twenty

Beth rushed into the bedroom where Kevin dozed under a Hudson Bay blanket, jaunty with its stripes of green and scarlet, gold and navy blue. His portable radio played classical music—Brahms, she thought—softly in the background. He was always careful, bringing fresh batteries whenever they went on a trip anywhere.

"Kevin, wake up."

He moaned and rolled over. "What now?"

"Someone tried to kill David."

He bolted upright and swung his feet to the ground. "What?"

"Someone—"

"Yes, I heard you. How? How is he? "

"Poisoned with something. Anne gave him an antidote and she and Thomas are with him now."

"Who told—"

"Mike."

"For God's sake, stay here with me. Don't go wandering all over the house."

He rubbed his face with his long fingers and shook his head.

"You need to stay awake. All you've done here is nap."

"Between the murder and your scrapping family, it seemed the best thing to do."

He held up one arm, she plopped down beside him, and snuggled. What if someone killed him? What would she do without him?

As though he read her mind, he said, "We'll take care of each other, Beth. Don't worry about me."

"I can't lose you," she said, her head buried in his sweater.

"Nor I, you. Have you been to see your mother?"

"No."

"Why don't we go see how she's doing?"

A few moments later, they knocked on the door of Andrea's room.

Anne sat at David's bedside and took his vital signs every few minutes. When his pulse slowed, and the pauses in his breathing lengthened, she used another of her store of Narcan, injecting into his thigh this time.

"How is he?" said Thomas when he walked in a few minutes later.

"Better after that last one. I think he's waking up."

Thomas came over from his chair by the window and stood with his hand on Anne's shoulder. She reached up and held on to his strong fingers. How comforting to have him with her, she thought. How safe. But they would have to keep each other safe until they escaped this awful house. And the only way to do that was to identify the killer. This attempt on David changed everything. Perhaps together, she and Thomas could investigate.

She didn't want to, but they would have to, for their own sakes and for the others, especially the children. A cold ripple of fear crossed her back. Every time they interfered with a killer's plans, death neared for one of them. The last time she faced a professional killer but persuaded her to run rather than shoot. But this killer was likely an amateur and so far, unpredictable.

"Anne?"

David's voice croaked from the bed, and she rushed over to him. A faint stain of pink relieved the pallor of his face.

"I'm here."

His eyes focussed on her this time, and his pupils reacted quickly to the light. "What happened to me?"

"Someone poisoned you with an opioid."

His dark eyebrows knitted, almost meeting in the middle over a deep furrow and his mouth formed a thin, hard line. "What? Why?"

"Someone here wanted both of you dead."

Anger bubbled into his words. "But why the hell?"

She didn't want to upset him any more than she already had.

"We can think about that later. Right now, I want you to rest. I'll stay right here."

His face, again pale and wan against the sheets and taut with fear, stared up at her."What if whoever it is, comes again?"

"We'll be here," said Thomas.

"Mike needs help. The wood was getting low again."

"He's right. I'll stay here with the door locked. We'll be fine," said Anne.

She hoped they'd be fine and that whoever was killing was cowardly, needing his victims comatose before he confronted them. Thomas kissed Anne lightly, and she locked the door behind him.

"Why would someone want to kill both of us?"

Anne sat beside him again and took his hand. "Why do people kill? Revenge, money, hate, love: so many motives."

David shook his head, furrowed his forehead again, but tears welled up in his eyes. "But why Vanessa?"

Why anyone, Anne thought. Why this kind man who loved children and wanted a family?

"Revenge for Karen's death? Making you suffer?"

He shook his head again. "That would be Brad or Andrea or Trevor."

"What do you have that any of these people want? What plan did Vanessa interfere with?"

"She had no involvement with my business. She was going to be my wife and the mother of the children once the adoption went through."

"You planned to adopt together?"

"I planned it that way. Her attitude towards the children and the dogs shocked me this weekend."

He turned his head away from her. Hiding his sorrow or his anger?

"Will someone contest the adoption?"

"Andrea and Brad. Andrea loves Hamish, but only Hamish, not Olivia. Brad doesn't give a damn about Hamish but does about his share of the trust money. I think they plan to petition the court."

"If they can proceed legally, why would they kill Vanessa?"

"The court would look more favourably on a married couple."

"I suppose. Hamish as a motive for murder. How horrible. Someone has a twisted mind."

A spasm of pain passed over David's face.

"What is it? Are you getting some discomfort?"

"The thought of not being a father to those kids, Anne. It's all I ever wanted. Because my dad wasn't involved with me until I was a teen, I missed a family life. My mother married, but my step-father didn't like me, and I came to live with my dad when I was fourteen. I don't want that for Hamish and Olivia. I look after Nicholas, but he's almost a grown man. He lived with us sometimes when he was younger, but mostly with his mother. Neither Hamish nor Olivia have mothers. I hoped to give them one."

"You'll be successful, I'm sure. After all, you're their brother, and I'm sure you'll meet someone who will love the children."

"Trevor is their uncle."

"Carmel is mentally ill."

Carmel. A twisted, broken mind. But she seemed so fragile and so weak, not a planner. Anne couldn't see hers as the brain behind the poisonings and that vicious attack on Vanessa.

David drifted back to sleep, leaving Anne alone with her thoughts. A family life. That's what she would give up if she said no to Thomas. He loved her, but would he stay with her if she didn't marry him? He had a conventional family life with his first wife and his children and his mother, and he wanted her to be part of his life now. Although being a part-time CIA agent or asset was hardly conventional. And why was she saying no after all? Politics? Was she going to let a temporary aberration in the USA keep her from being with the man she loved? And he said they could live anywhere. Perhaps a few months a year in Vermont would be okay.

She had friends there, and Vermont was more like Canada than other places. He had a condo in New York, and that, too, would be exciting. And she would be with Thomas, who loved her. And his family, most of them, had come around to accepting her since the grandmother died. And she loved his grandchildren, and they would be the children she never had.

Why was she so stubborn? Later, when David recovered, she would tell Thomas that she wanted to make a life with him. Later, when they weren't boxed up with a killer. She glanced out the window. Still snowing. Was this intolerable weekend ever going to end?

She jerked upright when the doorknob moved.

"Who is it?"

No one answered.

She listened at the door for a moment and sat down to read, but her heart pounded. She got up to wander the room again, hurrying to the bedside when David spoke to her.

"Anne."

He sat up in bed and rubbed his face with his hands as though wiping away a veil. His blue eyes gazed back at her from his now ruddy face; the shadows were gone.

"How are you?"

"Fine, I think. As though I had a great sleep. How long have I been out?"

"Just an hour this time."

"What happened to me? Did you say opioid?"

"Yes, someone fed you opioid."

Shock but no guilt flashed across his face. His eyes rounded and he tilted his head to one side. "Narcotic?"

"Yes."

"But why? But who?"

His confusion was genuine, Anne thought. "We don't know. Who would want both you and Vanessa gone? Who inherits from you?"

"The children and Vanessa."

"Vanessa by name in your will?"

His forehead wrinkled in a frown, and his mouth drew into a thin, hard line. He was quick, Anne thought.

"Yes. I was going to change it after we were married to say "my wife, Vanessa McKnight", but as of right now it reads Vanessa Donland."

"Who inherits from her?"

"I have no idea. Vanessa said she didn't need a will, that she had nothing to leave."

"You have to make a will right now."

"No lawyers here."

"A holographic one will stand until this horror is over."

"Can you hand me some paper from the desk?"

She opened the roll-top desk in the corner near the window, took a few pieces of letter-sized bond from a stack and a pen, and brought them to him.

"I think you should include provision for the guardianship of the children. It may be that one or more of these people want Hamish and the money that comes with him."

"My God. You think that's the motive?"

"We have to consider it."

"Can you bring me something to write on? There's an atlas on the shelf."

Anne found the blue National Geographic atlas and laid it across David's knees.

He wrote steadily for fifteen minutes. When he finished, he

sighed. "For the time this will is in effect, I've made you and Thomas and my personal lawyer the guardians and the trustees for Hamish, Olivia and Nicholas. I left everything to them and Nicholas in equal shares. They get their shares in turn when they reach twenty-five and generous support before that. I left some money to Eloise. Is that okay with you?"

Anne raised her eyebrows in surprise. Was there no one closer to him?

"I'm not sure we are the correct people for the long term, but for this weekend, that should work, since you've included the lawyer. What about witnesses? Whom do you want?"

"Trevor and Mike."

"I'll find them later. I'm going to the playroom to ask Eloise to sit with you for a little. I don't want to leave you here for very long."

"Where's Thomas?"

Anne stood with her hand on the doorknob to answer. "Wood-gathering with Mike."

"Right. Lock the door behind you, will you?" David said.

He fished his key ring out of his pocket and tossed it to her.

"Of course."

Anne walked down the hall to the children's room, knocked, and went in. The children both slept, Hamish in his crib, hugging his stuffed elephant, Olivia, her blanket clutched in her hand. Eloise smiled at her from the rocking chair.

"I think David would like to see you," Anne said.

Eloise's face glowed with her delighted smile. "I'll go now if you can stay with the children?"

"Of course," Anne said and slipped into the rocking chair drawn up beside the crib.

Hamish slept with his bottom in the air. Across the room, Olivia stirred in her bed, rolled over, and took a tighter hold on her blanket.

Eloise turned on the intercom and tip-toed out of the room and down the hall. She tapped on David's door.

"Who is it?"

"Eloise."

"Just a moment."

David crawled out of bed, stood up, wobbled, and walked over to the door and unlocked it. "Come in."

He teetered, and she tucked under his arm to support him back to bed.

"Lock the door," he said.

"Certainly, but why?"

She clicked the lock and sat beside him in the armchair Anne left by the bed.

"Are the children alone?"

"No, no. Anne is with them for a few minutes."

"Someone tried to kill me."

Her dark eyes rounded, and fear erased her happy smile. "What? Why?"

"Anne thinks someone wants to eliminate people who might claim Hamish and his trust money."

Her eyes filled with tears, and she grasped his hand where it lay on the blue bedspread. His fingers closed over hers, and a wave of longing flooded her heart. She took a long breath. "Do you know who? Or do Anne and Thomas?"

"They suspect everyone, I think. Even me."

"And me. I would adopt the children in a heartbeat, but I love them. I wouldn't deprive them of you. And why would you poison yourself?"

"Throw them off the track, I suppose."

She shook her head. How could he think that about himself? He was such a good man. "You've been reading too many mysteries. People don't poison themselves in real life. It's too risky. I'm sure they don't suspect you. But me—"

"No one who knows you would think you would kill anything.

You're the most loving person I know. I'm sorry that Vanessa treated you so badly. Do you know—"

His voice broke, and he turned away his face.

"Know what?"

"It seems she was my half-sister."

His half-sister. He must be sick with shame. His eyes held tears when he looked at her again and pleaded for understanding. She squeezed his fingers and nodded. "How awful for you."

"It makes me feel as though I'd committed incest."

He would take the blame on himself rather than on that witch. She fought to control her anger. David didn't need her rage; he needed her understanding. "Unknowingly."

They sat with their hands clasped together as the faint light from the window faded. Shadows deepened and soon a narrow pool of yellow light from the oil lamp at the bedside, isolated them from the darkness, surrounding them with safety.

She loved him so much. What would he say; what would he do, if she were to tell him? Could she ever tell him or would he think that she, too, wanted his money? Presently, David slept, and she leaned back in her chair and watched the slight movements of his chest.

The faint sounds of a child whispering came over the monitor. Eloise slipped away, setting the lock in the doorknob behind her.

When Eloise returned, Anne went down to the kitchen where she stoked the fire in the wood stove and put a kettle of snow, left for her by one of the men, on the burner to melt. Ice on the window darkened the room, and the supply of oil for the lamps was running low. Quite a store of batteries in the pantry, she thought, some for the larger lanterns that should last until the power came on and they escaped from here. What of their decision to investigate? Were they getting anywhere?

She created a list of the suspects in her mind but stumbled over the question on motive. Hamish, either because someone wanted a child or because someone wanted a trust fund could be one. Revolting.

What about hate? Who would hate Vanessa and David that much? Karen's family? Brad or Andrea or Beth? Somehow she couldn't see them as having that much rage. Andrea was a foolish and impetuous drunk but basically loved Hamish.

Brad, now. Perhaps he was greedy for money? Perhaps he was broke and this was the only way out? And Beth? She and Kevin appeared to be stable and sensible, but she knew nothing about their finances or their desire or ability to have children for that matter.

Mike and Thomas came in, interrupting her thoughts. She told Mike that David wanted him to witness a document.

"Why me?"

"That's what he wants. Trevor as well. Finish your tea and come up. I'll tell Trevor."

She tapped at Trevor's door and she explained what David wanted.

"I'll be right there."

When she unlocked the door to David's room, his eyes popped open, and a spasm of fear crossed his face. His fists curled where they lay on the blanket.

"It's Anne, David."

His hands relaxed, and he closed his eyes again. "Eloise was here."

She heard the longing in his voice.

"I know. I stayed with the children."

"I didn't tell her how I felt."

"Do you know how you feel?"

He turned anxious eyes towards her. "I think so."

"Not rebound?"

"No, I think I've loved her a long time but Vanessa—the glamour, the...seduction..."

"Perhaps you should give it a little time?"

"I've known her a long time, Anne. I don't want to lose her."

He shook his head and took a long breath. "Did you find Trevor and Mike?"

"They're coming."

Anne brought the atlas back to David, who placed the document, with only the signature page revealed, for both men to sign.

When they came in, David showed them the document, and first, he signed and then they did. Only Mike asked a question.

"What—"

"Business," David said.

The two men left Anne and David alone. When he opened his mouth to speak, Anne put her finger to her lips and opened the door. Trevor lingered in the hallway.

"Was there something?" she said.

He flushed and stammered his answer. "No, no. Just tying my shoe."

He trotted off down the hall to his own room. Anne came back to the bedside.

"What do you want to do with it?" she said.

"Lock it in the desk. When I can get up, I'll put it in the safe."

"Let me scan it first."

She used a scanning app on her phone and saved the will. When the internet returned, she would send it to David.

He handed her a key from his bedside table, and she put the will in the middle of a stack of business papers and told him what she had done.

"Are you going to tell them?"

"Yes, at dinner."

"I hope that takes a target off your back."

"It might put one on yours."

Anne shuddered. Not again. But this had to be done to protect the children.

She returned to the kitchen for some tea to carry to Carmel.

Chapter Twenty-One

B ack in the kitchen, Anne boiled the kettle again and made yet another pot of tea. She added water and coffee to the white percolator. When the men came in, brushing the snow off their clothes, the table was set with mugs, milk, and sugar.

Someone that worked for David was a baker, Anne thought, as she placed homemade blueberry muffins and ginger crackle cookies on a china plate. The pattern of old-fashioned pink roses on the gold-rimmed china, similar to one her mother had used, matched the mug she'd carried up to Carmel.

Thomas, his dark hair damp from the snow, pushed up the sleeves of his navy sweater and sat. "How are all your patients," he asked, reaching for a muffin.

"Hamish is okay between bouts of coughing, as long as we keep up his inhalers. Fortunately, Eloise got an extra refill when they came up here. Andrea is not as well. I gave her an oral antibiotic, but she needs intravenous, I think. Carmel's holding her own, but it's only a matter of time before she slips into a coma. She drank a cup of tea with milk and ate half of a cracker, but that's far from enough."

"And David?"

"Awake. I'm letting him up for dinner. But I need to get them all out of here. Andrea may deteriorate, and Carmel is in a dangerous state. I'm surprised there's no satellite phone here."

"There is," said Mike, "But no charge and the battery is an odd one."

He slathered butter on his third muffin and scarfed it down. Worked hard and ate to match, Anne thought.

"No one here was ever a ham radio buff, I suppose," Thomas said.

"The old man was."

"Cooper?"

"No, the guy who built this place and sold it to Cooper."

"I thought Copper built it," said Thomas.

"Naw. Cooper renovated it and added all the geegaws and extra bathrooms, but old man Stanley built it in the thirties."

"And he was a ham radio operator."

"Had a license and used to talk to folks all over."

"But why would it still be here?" Anne said.

"He left a bunch of stuff in the attic, and when they renovated, they pulled it all out. Cooper wasn't here, and when they finished, I loaded it back in. Bunch of junk, mostly."

"Could we search?" said Thomas.

"Why not? After we finish these muffins. That Cassie sure can bake."

"Cassie's the cook here?" said Anne.

"Ya. She's a crackerjack."

Later, Anne cleared up while the men searched the attic. Another meal coming. Every time she came up here, she ended up in the kitchen. Containers of pasta sauce were stacked in one corner. That would do.

After a cursory knock, Beth strode into her mother's room. Why give him a head's up? Kevin followed her in. Her mother lay propped up on pillows, her breathing coming in rapid shallow gasps, her lips tinged with blue. But she was so ill. When did this happen?

Beth stood over her brother, her arms folded tight against her chest. "How long has she been like this?"

Brad didn't look at her but kept his eyes on his mother. "Not long. Anne is treating her for pneumonia."

"What with?"

"What with? Why? What they treat pneumonia with. A shot of something. Antibiotic, I think, and her puffers."

"What puffers?"

His mouth hardened to a thin line. "What the hell, Beth? Do you never ask her about her health, about who she sees, and what she takes?"

"Why would I? She doesn't remember."

Andrea opened her eyes and stared at Beth. "Yes, I—"

"Don't talk, Mom. Wait until you're better."

"I want to talk to you," Beth said to Brad, tugging at his arm.

He shook her off. "Keep your hands to yourself."

He walked away from the bedside and stood in the window.

"Too close—"

"Her hearing's poor. What do you want?"

"We have to commit her to a facility before she kills herself or someone else. Does she still drive?"

"Christ, Beth. She may not survive this. Can't we talk about this when we're back in the city? What's the matter with you?"

His face, dark with rage, hovered over her. She stepped back, glancing at the bed where Kevin was holding her mother's hand and speaking softly to her. He was such a good man, so much better than she was.

"Nothing. I don't want Mom to die, and I want her to find help for her addiction."

"Is that all you can think about? Her addiction, her alcoholism, her obsession with Hamish. You never stop."

"And all you have done is nothing, and it's come to this."

Beth stared into her brother's eyes, mirrors for her own.

"Could you two pipe down," Kevin said.

He stood up and took Beth's hand. "We should go. Your mom's exhausted and needs to sleep."

"Don't come back unless you want to support her."

She whirled to confront her brother. "I—"

"Not now, Beth," said Kevin. He closed the door behind them.

Chapter Twenty-Two

A nne tapped on Andrea's door and walked in. In his chair beside the fire, Brad shook his bovine head. His red-rimmed eyes over swollen cheeks entreated Anne. "She's no better. What can we do?"

"I'll give her another shot of antibiotic now, and if she's able, you encourage her to drink, even sips will help if they're frequent enough. She doesn't have any heart issues, does she?"

"I don't know."

"I'll check her medicine cabinet."

A drugstore-worth of prescription medications tumbled out when she opened the door of the cabinet. Most of them were psychotropics of one sort or another—anti-depressives, anxiolytics, sleeping pills. Many containers were almost full and had different doctors' names. She spent a lot of time trying to feel better, Anne thought. One prescription stood out—oxycontin, responsible for an epidemic of addiction. Half of the pills were missing, but the date was a month or so prior.

"Brad, can you come in here?"

"What's the matter?" he said, leaning with arms propped on the door frame.

"She was on all these meds?"

She gestured at the vials and bottles lined up on the counter, and he picked up a random medication, set the vial down, and picked up another. He shook his head again. "Christ, no. What are they all for?"

"Mostly depression, and anxiety. None cardiac. She's been doctor-shopping."

"What?"

"Seeing different doctors and getting different meds from each of them. One of them gave her oxycontin."

"Oxycontin. Isn't that—"

"Yes. One of the ones implicated in the addiction epidemic. But only about half of them are missing, and the prescription is old. Did you know she had it?"

"No, no. Why do you ask that?"

"Something sedated David, perhaps these pills."

He gasped and stepped back from her, shaking his head. "No. No. I, we didn't do anything."

"Does she take oxy?"

He shook his head again. "No. Mom prefers booze to pills. She told me she'd rather be drunk than stoned."

"I don't see anything to treat a heart condition, but she uses puffers. Did she smoke?"

"Up to about five years ago."

"Did her doctor say she had chronic lung disease."

"He said chronic bronchitis."

Anne checked the vials of pills for the most recent dates and dumped the rest into the wastebasket and carried it with her into the bedroom. Andrea stirred.

"Andrea," Anne said. "Can you talk to me?"

A paroxysm of coughing turned Andrea's lips blue. Anne put an arm around her, sat her further up in bed and tucked another pillow behind her back.

When Andrea's gasping changed to harsh, regular breaths, Anne said, "Do you take all the pills in your cabinet, Andrea?"

"Only Doctor Bassett's," she said, her words coming in harsh gasps.

Doctor Bassett's were the latest and included Oxycontin.

"Only one more question. Are you taking Oxycontin?"

"Some, but none this week."

"Okay. I'm going to give you another needle."

Anne shot another dose of antibiotic into Andrea's wasted thigh. The skin, wrinkled and soft, was that of a much older woman.

Andrea closed her eyes and relaxed back into the higher pillow. Anne drew Brad across the room. "She's struggling, but I'm afraid to give her morphine, not knowing what she's taken already. Stay with her and if she worsens call me."

"What do I look for?"

"Longer coughing spells, blue spells, more difficulty breathing. I'll be back."

"Can't you stay?"

"I'm checking on Hamish and Carmel. They're sick too."

She paused at the door. Brad held his mother's hand and folded over it, laying his forehead against her palm. She hadn't seen that sort of emotion from him before.

She needed to talk to Thomas about the Oxycontin.

Anne tapped on the door of the children's room and peered into the room.

"Come in," said Eloise.

She sat in a rocking chair with Olivia, who held a Doctor Seuss book in her lap. *Green Eggs and Ham*. The children in Anne's practice liked that one. It had even encouraged one boy to learn to read. It was a proud moment for both of them when he read aloud.

"Shush," said Olivia with one pudgy finger to her lips. "Hamish is sleeping."

"I'll be very quiet."

Anne tiptoed to the crib. Hamish lay with one arm outstretched, the other clutching a teddy bear with one floppy ear. A bandage covered the other side of its head. The baby breathed quietly, with no audible wheeze.

"How long has he been better?" she asked.

"About an hour, " Eloise said and tucked the blanket around the little boy.

"Don't let him oversleep the time for his puffers. You can try to give them to him without waking him, if you like."

"He'll wake up soon, I think."

"Can you come into the bathroom with me?"

"Certainly," said Eloise in a puzzled voice. "You stay here and watch Hamish, Olivia."

"But—"

"Please."

Inside the bathroom, Anne asked, "Where do you keep the medications?"

"Here."

Eloise brought out a large, grey lockbox from inside the under-sink cabinet and opened it with a key she kept on a chain around her neck.

"You're quite careful."

"Yes, I keep my medications in here as well—aspirin and Tylenol threes for migraine."

"Could you check everything is there?"

Eloise placed all the prescriptions on the counter and handed Anne the vial of Tylenol threes.

"You haven't used many of these."

"I haven't had a headache for some time. Are you looking for something that sedated Vanessa?"

"Yes."

"I didn't kill her, Anne. I didn't."

Her voice broke, and tears filled her brown eyes.

"I have to check everywhere."

"Yes."

At the door to the bathroom, Olivia scowled at Anne.

"Why did you make Eloise cry?" she said. "I thought you were nice."

"It's all right," said Eloise. "Anne is nice. She didn't make me cry. Aren't you watching Hamish?"

"He woke up, and he wants his bottle."

"I'm coming."

She scooped the medications back in the box and locked it.

"Is that all?"

"I'll check Hamish's chest, now that he's up."

The baby still breathed too rapidly but didn't struggle as much. A few wheezes remained in his lungs.

"Not too bad. Keep up the puffer, every one-two hours now."

"I will."

Eloise lifted Hamish into her arms and settled back into the rocking chair.

At the door, Anne paused. They were safe for now. She turned the thumb lock in the door handles and ran down to the kitchen to get some food for Carmel.

Thomas and Mike climbed the oak stairs, the treads worn by the passage of almost ninety years, to the door to the attic. Faint echoes of green paint clung to the old wood. An iron key of ancient design hung on a wooden peg. Mike turned the key; the lock protested with a metallic screech.

Inside, dust motes, disturbed by their feet, floated like fireflies in light from a south window. Stacks of crates, some wooden, some cardboard, lined the room. Abandoned desks, lamps, even an elegant side-board in mahogany leaned against each other in a pile in the centre.

"Where did you stash it?" said Thomas.

"I loaded the boxes near the door last, and I think that's where the old equipment is."

They searched, Thomas at one end of the stack, Mike at the other.

In one box, labelled *fine dishes*, Thomas found a set of twelve plates in an art deco design. He turned one over and read Clarice Cliff, May Avenue. The pattern resembled that painting Anne liked so much—Street in Glen William by a Canadian artist. A curving street and trees in autumn oranges and yellows. Anne would know something about the porcelain too. In other boxes, he found more of the same pattern, including a tea set. Perhaps he would buy the china from David when this was over, a gift for Anne.

"Tom."

"Yeah."

"I found it."

A battered black metal box and a freestanding microphone sat in a wooden crate.

"Think it might work?"

"The old man was using the equipment the day he died so it should."

"The day he died?"

"Yeah. The cops found him slumped over in front of the microphone. He was ninety years old."

"No suggestion he died from electrocution, then."

"Hell, no."

Mike carried the box down to the living room and set up in the front window. Cold air seeped through the frame and under the window. Upkeep a bit behind, Thomas thought. Did David need money? He didn't think so. Likely more time.

"Why in here?"

"Open to the north. Maybe we'll get lucky if we can charge her up."

"What kind of battery?"

"Just your regular twelve-volt."

"Is it in the box?"

"Naw. I took it home. Wouldn't have lasted up there and that seemed like a waste. Coop said I could take what I could use."

Anne called Thomas from the doorway to the kitchen. "Can you come out here for a moment."

The swinging door closed behind her. When he came through, she stood at the window, peering at the falling snow and shaking her head.

"What's up?"

"I went through Andrea's stock of pills and found multiple prescriptions for psychotropic medications, from different doctors and pharmacies. A doctor-shopper. One is a bottle of Oxycontin. It's possible it was used to sedate Vanessa and David."

"Or any of the others?"

"Yes, she had quite a selection. Brad's surprise seemed genuine."

"What did you do with them?"

She pointed to a bag on the counter that bulged with bottles, vials, blister packs, and unopened boxes.

"You weren't kidding. What are you going to do with them?"

"Hide them in the pantry. No one else is interested in cooking. Eloise has some Tylenol three's for migraine."

"Did you take those too?"

"She's not my patient. Andrea is."

She put her hand on his arm and cocked her head at him.

"We should go over what we know."

"Later. Mike and I found the ham radio set and are going to see if we can get it working."

"What are the problems?"

"No battery, for a start."

"If you need something, I'll search if you want."

Thomas nodded and pushed through the door into the living room. He had to take her out of there and back to their lives, so she could make her decision.

Chapter Twenty-Three

Anne carried a cup of tea and a quarter-piece of toast upstairs and along the hall to Carmel's room. Trevor's flaming red hair identified him in the dim light from the windows at either end of the hall. He stood with his hand on his bedroom door and waited for Anne. "Did you see her?"

"Yes. She ate a small cracker and drank some tea. I'm going to try again now."

"Should I come in?"

"Yes, but let me be the one to be firm with her. And don't interrupt."

He opened his mouth to protest but shut it when Anne shook her head at him.

Inside, she placed the tea and toast beside Carmel's bed and stepped back while Trevor whispered to his wife. Carmel lay still, her eyes focussed on the ceiling or something beyond. He kissed her forehead and perched beside her, holding her hand. "Sweetheart, Anne is here to see you again."

She turned her eyes towards him but didn't move in the bed. "She made me drink some tea. With milk. What if I gain?"

"Don't worry. Anne knows what you are afraid of, and she won't make you eat too much. Trust her, Carmel. She's a children's doctor and very kind."

"Will she help us with Hamish when we take him home."

"She'll help with all our children."

He turned back to Anne, tears rolling over his freckled face. "Please."

"Carmel, I want you to sit up now. Trevor will help you."

Trevor lifted her shoulders and tucked pillows behind her. Anne sat on the bed with a half-full cup of tea.

"I brought you some fresh tea."

"I'm not thirsty."

"Of course, you're not. Your body is confused and can't tell thirsty from not thirsty. But I've been keeping track, and I understand how much you should be drinking. Here you go."

Carmel took a reluctant sip from the cup and offered it back to Anne.

"Some more and then I have a triangle of toast for you."

"Bread is the worst. I'll—"

"No, you won't. Remember you have to eat or no one will let you adopt."

"You'll tell them I'm okay."

"No, I won't, unless you are eating and drinking more. Try again."

Anne gave her back the cup. After Carmel sipped twice and pushed the cup back at her, Anne handed her the toast.

"No."

"Yes."

Carmel nibbled, swallowed, twisted her upper lip as though something dreadful fouled the toast, and swallowed. "I can't—"

"You must."

Afterwards, back in the hall, Anne said, "Stay with her for the next hour. I don't want her to vomit that up. I'll be back."

"Thank you, thank you."

"You're welcome. Now go back in."

Back in the kitchen, she wondered where he had been before she encountered him in the hall. In fact, where had he been most of the afternoon?

Mike and Thomas set up the old ham radio set on a card table in the living room. Faint light from the ice-laden window fell across the temporary work-bench.

"I'll get a lantern," said Mike.

By the time he returned, Thomas had set up the equipment. Dials were located on the front of a battered black-metal box. Tethered to it were a telegraph key, a loudspeaker and a microphone. A connection snaked out from the back for a battery. Mike shone the light on the wire. "So what will we do for a battery?" he said.

"How many volts?"

"Anything up to twelve, but I couldn't find any in the workroom in the basement."

"What about in the shed?"

"Naw."

Thomas rocked back on his heels.

"What about the ATVs," he said.

"We made need them to get out when the storm passes."

"We won't draw much, and only two of us need to go."

"Which two?"

"Decide later."

"I'll pull a battery out of the small one."

Thomas waited. What about Anne's decision? Could he live in Canada most of the time? The property in Vermont weighed on his mind. The simplest thing to do was gift it to Daniel and the girls, but they wanted him to live there, to be there when they wanted to come home. That was not going to happen, even if he retired. He could run the business from Toronto and New York. Would Anne agree to that? He could install a caretaker couple in the house in Culver's Mills.

Mike pushed through the door from the kitchen carrying the battery.

"Here goes," he said when he connected the wires and flipped the switch. Static roared out of the speaker.

"We're in business," Thomas said.

Back in their bedroom, Beth slumped into a low chair near the fireplace. Kevin stirred up the embers and, when flames licked upwards, added birch bark and two pieces of cedar, shims from some construction project; the room filled with the warming scent of burning maple and the comforting crackling of the flames. She leaned back and closed her eyes as the warmth of the fire floated over her.

"Every time," she said. "Every time I try to talk to Brad about Mom, he turns it on me. What I haven't done. How badly I've treated her. How about how she treated me?"

"What has she done, Beth?"

"She's a drunk and an embarrassment—"

"No, love. What has she done to you? To hurt you, not herself."

Beth's tears flooded down her face.

"She never loved me. Just Brad, and now Hamish. Not me and certainly not Olivia. Nothing I did was ever enough. I wasn't smart enough, or pretty enough, or popular enough. And now I haven't any children, and she takes that as a personal affront."

"Why?"

"She wants a dynasty to continue Dad's name."

"That's a bit strange since it's not even her family."

Beth went on, lost in her memories of childhood.

"She always drank too much, always humiliating me in front of my friends. No one wanted to come to my house. Brad's friends did. But they laughed at her and Brad never understood that."

Kevin drew her up from the chair and sat beside her on the bed. She sobbed against his shoulder.

"You felt she didn't value you?"

"I know she doesn't. She never said she loved me. Not once. Not ever. Not in a note, not on a card, not to my face. Never."

"We don't have to visit anymore. Whatever you want to do."

"I don't know. I don't know."

"I love you."

"And I love you and your mom and dad, and your sisters."

"They want to be your family, but you've kept them at arm's length."

"Afraid."

"Afraid?"

"Of rejection, I guess. But I'll try to move past that feeling."

She clung to him, breathed in his familiar fragrance of leather and some sort of spice and something just him, safe and secure. Her pain drifted away. She jolted out of the drowsy haze. They still had to do something about Andrea.

Andrea's struggling gasps filled the room with pain. Brad sat beside her as the frail chest rose, and he waited for the gasp that would take in her next breath. How had it come to this? She was well when they arrived. Was she? He shook his head. He was going to lose her and Beth blamed him. Blamed him for not helping her with the drinking problem. Her addiction. He needed to face it. She ran into the storm with a little child, and that was on him. He bought the booze she guzzled day and night. That was on him, too. And he fed her paranoid fantasy about David. She and he couldn't look after a small child.

He plodded to the window, a heavy weight bearing down on his shoulders. What should he do? He couldn't tell her there was no hope. No hope for her to get Hamish and her plan for Carmel to adopt the boy was foolish. Carmel couldn't look after a guppy. She might die, too.

Behind him, Andrea called out. "Brad? Where?"

"I'm here, Mom."

He sat down beside her and took her hand.

"Beth?"

"She went back to her room."

"Tell her..."

The faint voice trailed off.

"Tell her what?"

But she was gone again. Why had she always favoured him over Beth? He knew it, and Beth knew it, and it poisoned their relationship. And Beth was right. They had to help her with the drinking if she survived this. He didn't think Anne had much hope. What had she meant, telling him to be hopeful? Not about Hamish. Likely about survival.

"I do love her."

Her voice, suddenly strong, startled him and he jerked his head up to look at her. But she had drifted away. Perhaps he would be able to tell Beth that, sometime? Perhaps, they could search together for somewhere she could go to help her recover? She hadn't had a drink for a while now. How long until the DT's?

"I'll tell her."

Andrea moaned, opened her pale, swollen eyelids, but the watery blue eyes focussed somewhere beyond him and closed again.

How long? How much longer? His fists knotted until the fingers turned white.

Chapter Twenty-Four

Anne rang the dinner bell at 6:00 pm. Those who weren't sick trailed in, first Mike and Thomas, after them, Brad and finally Trevor, Eloise, Olivia and Hamish. David clattered down the stairs, bringing up the rear.

"I'll take a plate up to Andrea after dinner," said Brad.

His eyes, outlined in brown circles of exhaustion, focussed on Eloise when she spoke.

"How is she?" asked Eloise.

Her face reflected her genuine concern, Anne thought.

"About the same. Still coughing and not able to talk much."

"Poor soul."

Mike and Thomas sat down and reached for the biscuits filling a basket. Crumbs tumbled over Mike's plaid shirt and he brushed them off with a lazy hand. "You baked these?" Mike said.

"Yes."

"Better than the cook's."

A steaming casserole of chilli, the biscuits, and a bowl of vegetables filled the centre of the table.

"To the cook," said David, raising his glass of red wine.

"Thanks, but most of it was Cassie's work."

When was David going to get to it, Anne wondered. He said he was going to tell them he changed his will. Now he was delaying, making toasts and feeding the baby. She glanced at him and raised her eyebrows. He grimaced and nodded. "Before you all leave, I want to tell you something. One of you tried to kill me today."

Anne searched for a reaction, anything to indicate who might have a guilty conscience, but nothing.

"I decided that one motive could be money, mine and the trust for the children so I changed my will."

"No lawyers here," said Trevor.

"I don't need a lawyer for a holographic will. You witnessed it, you and Mike."

"That was a will? I—"

"I left the bulk of my estate to the children in trust and named Anne and Thomas and my city accountant as trustees and guardians of the children. No one need think that any action taken this weekend will change that. If I am killed before we get out of here, Anne and Thomas will take the children and Eloise with them. Do I make myself clear?"

"Don't matter a damn to me," said Mike, spooning another helping of chilli onto his plate and liberating another biscuit from the wicker basket beside him.

"Why do you trust Eloise?" said Trevor. "A blind man could see she wants the kids and you and your money. Maybe she—"

"Non, non," said Eloise.

Her eyes filled with tears and she wrapped her arms around Hamish.

"No further discussion," said David. "Brad, I think you wanted to take some food to Andrea. What about Carmel?"

"Who made you king?" muttered Brad.

"My house, my rules, and my life at stake."

"She doesn't want any food," said Trevor.

"That doesn't matter. I'll go up with you if some of you will clear up here," said Anne.

"Bien sûr," said Eloise.

Anne climbed the stairs behind Trevor, leaving behind the clatter of dishes and Hamish's happy babbling. How many more days could she keep the two women alive.

At the top of the stairs, she took the tray from Trevor and knocked on Andrea's door. Brad reached them before she could go in. "I'll take it, Anne. You go on to Carmel."

Thomas turned the dials on the radio while Mike worked at stringing a line for an antenna. "Where do you think you'll find an antenna?"

"There's an old tv antenna attached on the east side of the house. I'm not sure if the wires run in here, but if they don't, I'll gerry-rig something."

"Good idea. I'm getting a lot of static but no voice. Can you do morse code?"

"Nope. Just SOS."

Mike followed a wire from the television to a connection on the east wall of the living room. "This might be it."

"Do we need call letters?"

"Maybe. I think there was a notebook in the bottom of the box."

Thomas reached in and pulled out a small black notebook, its cover as battered as the radio case. Careful script filled each line. "Here it is. It's a list of people he reached, the dates and the times of day. Here are his call letters. VA3eew. The entries stop the year he died. He has a long list of Vermont call letters. One of them is for someone in Culver's Mills."

"Let's give it a try on an emergency channel. Does he have one of those listed?"

"52, 53, 55."

"Let's try the first one, and call the Culver's radio."

"Not much chance after all these years."

"What's the date?

"1952."

Thomas twisted the dial to channel 52 and said, "This is VA3EEw calling W1SAM."

He repeated the call and then tuned to channel 53 and tried again. "This is VA3EEW calling W1SAM. Over."

"This is W1SAM. Come in VA3EEW. Over."

"VA3EEW calling. Are you still in Culver's Mills? Over."

"W1SAM here. Yes. Over."

"Can you reach Culver's Police with a message and our call numbers? Name's Beauchamp. We're stranded in the ice storm. And there's been a murder. Over."

"A murder. What the hell? Can do. Stand by. Over and out."

Mike grinned and high-fived Thomas.

"Good job," Thomas said. "I have to talk to Anne. Will you keep trying in case the Culver's police call?"

"Will do."

Thomas took the stairs from the living room to the second floor but when he reached their room, Anne wasn't there. Likely in with Carmel, he thought and clattered back down to the radio.

Anne sat at Carmel's bedside, encouraging a few sips of soup and then a bite of bread and butter.

"Butter, ugh."

"You're still cold, Carmel. Your body temperature is too low and you need fuel, just like the fire does."

"I'm so tired."

Carmel's eyes, sunken and dark-rimmed, peered at Anne out of an emaciated face, old before its time, with knife-edge cheekbones and dry, flaking lips. Her skin clung to the bones.

"I know you are. Just a little more."

Why did that man not sit down, she thought, as Trevor paced the carpet behind her. When she gathered up the dishes and carried the tray to the door, he was there to open it and followed her into the hall.

"What do you think you are doing?"

He loomed over her, his pale face bright red with fury.

"Feeding your wife."

"About the will."

"What about it?"

"You betrayed us. How did you and Thomas end up with Hamish?"

"We haven't. We're his guardians and trustees until David can pick someone else. And I never promised to acquire Hamish for you."

"You said she had to eat before we could adopt."

"Any child. And I expect when she has reached a normal weight, she'll get pregnant anyway."

"She'll get better when we have Hamish."

"Not going to happen."

He grabbed her arms but she pushed the tray against him, spilling soup and tea over his shirt and pants. Eloise opened the door to the playroom and popped her head out. "What's going on?"

"An accident. Could you bring me something to clean this up with?"

A moment later she handed Anne a roll of paper towels and Trevor stormed back into his room.

"What—"

"I'll tell you later," said Anne and returned to the kitchen with the remnants of the food and a pile of dirty paper.

Chapter Twenty-Five

———————

The desk sergeant called to Lieutenant Pete Graham's office across the wide squad room. Pete, a stocky, powerfully-built man with a buzz cut on his fair hair, picked up. "Yeah, Tony?"

"Guy on the phone says he took a call on his amateur radio from someone called Beauchamp. Beauchamp said he was stranded by the ice storm and that there was a murder."

"Where?"

"He didn't say but the call letters are Canadian."

"That's a long way for a ham radio signal."

"Storm effect, maybe."

"I'll call out to the house."

A maid answered and told Pete that Thomas Beauchamp was vacationing in Canada but she didn't know where and none of the family was home.

He walked across the room to where Brad, his resident technical genius, hunched over his computer. "Do you have a cell number for Thomas Beauchamp or Anne McPhail?"

"Yeah, both."

"Try to locate them and let me know."

After a few minutes, Brad's six-foot plus frame filled Pete's doorway. "Both off, boss."

"Can we use the radio to call on the amateur network?"

"Sure. What call letters?"

After half-an-hour, they gave up but asked the sergeant to monitor the band.

"I'll call Adam and see if he knows where they were going."

Adam was the former chief detective in Culver's Mills. Recently married, he and his wife were good friends of Anne McPhail and Thomas Beauchamp. He returned to school to do law and was recruited by the FBI.

"He's gone to Quantico, boss. They left last week."

"Already? I thought that wasn't until the new year."

"They moved it up."

"Erin go too?"

"Yeah. Maybe Catherine LaPlante?" Brad said.

Catherine Laplante, owner of a local bed and breakfast was also one of Anne's good friends. When she answered, Pete identified himself and asked his question.

Catherine said, "She hasn't found another body, has she?"

"Not as far as I know."

"She and Thomas were going to a lodge in Canada, near somewhere called Haliburton. One L. I think it's a private lodge."

"Do you know whose?"

"She said it was where they were involved in a murder investigation last winter. The owner died. What did she say his name was? Oh here it is. I have the number from that visit. I'd like to know if they're okay."

"Thanks. I'll let you know."

Pete swung his legs off his desk, hung up, and walked into the squad room. Brad raised his eyes from his monitor. "Any luck?"

"Yeah. I know about where they are. Now I want you to find out about a murder there last winter. After Christmas. I have the phone number of the lodge where it happened."

Again, Brad worked the keys on his computer. "Boss, the murder was reported at a place owned by a guy called Cooper Thwaite. He was the victim. I can get you the locale but the weather up there is ugly. No one's going in or out."

"Keep trying the radio."

"Nothing but static now."

"Keep listening."

In Bancroft, an OPP cruiser swung off the highway and down a small incline to the brick station. Family cars in the lot reminded him that the staff Christmas party was that day. He spotted his wife's car and smiled in anticipation of her tray of cookies and bars.

Inside, the constable on the desk called to him. "Sarg, I got a call from Vermont about a possible murder."

"Theirs or ours?"

"Ours."

"Why did they get it?"

"Apparently the lodge where it happened is iced in. Somewhere near the park," he said referring to the vast Algonquin Park south-west of Bancroft.

"Whose lodge?"

"Private. You remember the murder last winter of a guy called Thwaite?"

"Yeah?"

"Same place."

"What the hell? Can we reach them?"

"No way in, not even by sled. Lines down all over the place and heavy snow on top of the ice. Someone hooked up an amateur radio and called on an emergency channel to a Vermont radio they had the letters for. We have theirs."

"Have you tried—"

"Not yet."

"Go ahead."

He poured himself a coffee and scarfed down a square of matrimonial cake—his favourite, dates and oatmeal.

"No answer."

"Keep trying. What about a bird."

"Nothing doing yet."

"Let me know when they can get one in the air."

Mike stood another log on the sawed-off remains of a stately tree. He raised the ax high and bought it down with a satisfying crack, splitting the log in two. He stacked both on the pile behind him and steadied another. The killer walked past and loaded up with firewood.

"Glad you could make it," Mike said.

"What do you want?"

"To state my terms."

"Terms for what?"

"Don't play dumb. Terms to keep quiet about you and the knife. I know you killed her. It shouldn't be hard for a professional like yourself to hide an expenditure of say a thousand a week."

"A thousand a week. Are you nuts?"

"Sure, not that much for you, after you take the income tax deduction."

"Deduct blackmail?"

"Naw. Put me on the payroll as a helper or animal handler or something. Easy for you, easy for me."

"My accountant—"

"Works for you. I'll be along to see you when we get out of here. We reached the cops today. They'll be here as soon as the weather breaks."

"What will you—"

"Nothing, if we have a deal."

Mike shucked off his glove and stuck out a massive hand. "And oh, yeah. Behave as though nothing happened, even when we're alone."

The killer shook it and bolted away. Mike grinned, picked up his load of wood, and trudged back to the house.

Chapter Twenty-Six

Back in the kitchen, the killer sat at the scrubbed pine table and poured tea from a fat-bellied teapot. When Mike barged through the door with his load of wood, he held up a cup. "Tea?"

"Yeah, with milk and sugar."

Mike wolfed down a couple of cookies from a plate in the middle of the table. "Where is everyone?"

"Thomas is in the living room. The sick ones are in bed and the rest are with them or in their rooms."

"You keep tabs on everyone pretty good."

"I like to know what's going on."

"Sleepy."

"What's that?"

"Getting sleepy. Did you put—"

"What do you think," he said as Mike slumped over the table.

The killer struggled to pry Mike from his chair and drag him outside. He flopped him onto a sled and gasped for a few minutes with the work of moving the big man's dead weight. He pulled him away from the house and plodded across the field to the bush. Would someone see him? Who would? They were all busy with sick people or kids or that damn radio. He reached the forest and dragged the sled along for a few metres.

A work of a several moments left Mike face down on the snow, blood gushing from a wound in his neck, staining the pristine snow scarlet. Served him right, trying to blackmail him. The killer checked his clothes. Nothing. He dragged the sled to the shed, piled it with wood, and went back to the house.

He was stacking it in a neat row when Thomas opened the door. "Have you seen Mike?"

"Not for an hour or so when he brought in some logs. How's it going?"

"We reached the police in Culver's Mills and they called the OPP in Bancroft. They called us long enough for me to tell them about Vanessa before the signal cut out."

"Are they coming?"

"When the snow stops and they can get here. I told them about the downed wire. They'll bring a hydro crew with them."

"That's good news. How long?"

"No idea. How's the wood holding up?"

"What you see. We may have to cut up one of the downed trees."

Thomas went back in the house.

What would happen when the cops came and Thomas told them he saw him metres from the body? Maybe they would think Mike took off because he was the murderer. Yeah, that was what they would think. He trotted back up the stairs. Soon they would be out of here and they would have Hamish. But would they have to take him or would the courts give him up?

Chapter Twenty-Seven

Anne left her room carrying her battered leather medical bag. Someday, she would stop carting it around with her but she was happy she brought it with her this time. The only problem with the lodge design, she thought, as she contemplated the long dark hall, was the lack of windows in this space. Darkness swallowed the light from the single tall window at each end and the ornamental lanterns by the doors did little to alleviate the gloom.

What a place. If she were David, it would be on the market as soon as they got out of here. Three murders and an attempt, all in two years with the same people in the house. What would the police do? Would they be allowed to go home?

The next door along was Andrea's. She had her hand up to knock on the partially open door when Brad's voice came through.

"Don't worry, Mom. Hamish will be ours when we get out of here."

"How?"

The faint sound alarmed Anne but she hesitated. What would Brad say?

"Don't worry. I have a plan."

Anne knocked.

"Who is it? Mom's too ill to be disturbed."

Anne swung open the door and walked in the room. A single lamp at the bedside cast a rosy light on the pale, gasping woman in the bed. Anne pulled open the drapes at the window and turned on the overhead fixture.

"Why did you do that? She's tired."

"I have to be able to see her. Please turn off that lamp. The colour makes her look pinker than she is."

Anne examined Andrea, noting the blue tinge to her lips, her gasping respirations and the sibilant wheezes and coarse crackles in her chest. Andrea's eyes, full of fear, met hers and her cold, bony hand clutched at Anne's. "Am I—"

"You will be fine. I'm going to give you another shot of antibiotic and I want Brad to give you your puffers more often."

Andrea squeezed Anne's hand. After a moment, Anne freed herself and injected Andrea with antibiotic. She needed to talk to Brad. He sat a little distant, his eyes downcast and his hands curled into one another.

"Brad."

When he looked up, she jerked her head towards the door.

"How is she?" he said.

"Let's give her some quiet. You come outside with me."

"I'll be back in a minute, Mom. I want to talk to Anne."

In the hall, Brad slumped against the door and rubbed his face with his hands, knuckling away some tears. "She's dying, isn't she?"

"I don't know. She's gravely ill but she hasn't been on the antibiotic long. If we keep her going until rescue comes, I think she'll be okay."

"Thank you, thank you."

"Make sure you're hopeful with her."

"I'm trying."

He had a plan, she thought. What was it? But she had work to do and knocked at the door of the children's suite.

※

"Come in," called Eloise, after Anne knocked.

Eloise sat in the rocker with Olivia on her knees and a book propped against the arm. Hamish stirred in his crib. His respirations sounded easier, with no audible wheeze. At least one of her patients was improving, Anne thought.

"How is he?"

"Bien, Bien. He ate a little and he's been drinking."

"When was his last puffer?"

"About two hours ago."

Anne examined the little boy, checking his chest and his ears. Not much wheezing and no indication of pneumonia. "Fever this morning?"

"Thirty-eight Celsius when he woke up, but down since then."

"Good. I think he's on the mend. Keep up his puffers and let him up for a little while if he wants to."

Eloise sat back in the rocker and sighed. A tear rolled down her cheek.

Olivia reached up and brushed it away. "Don't cry, Eloise. Hamish is getting better," she said.

"I know."

"You love the children very much," Anne said. "How long have you been with them?"

"For four years. David's father hired me and after he died, David kept me on."

Something in the way she said David's name brought a smile to Anne's face. "How long have you loved him?"

Eloise swung her eyes to meet Anne's and then away. "From the first moment. But there is no hope."

"I wouldn't be so sure."

After a few more minutes of conversation, Anne left to attend her most difficult patient. Every time she went to Carmel's room, she expected the worst.

Before Anne reached Carmel's room, Thomas bounded up the back stairs and along the hall. "We have to talk. he said.

His dark eyes held that worried look that meant something had gone terribly wrong.

"What—"

"In our room.'"

"I have to see Carmel. I'll be quick."

"After, then."

She turned the knob and walked in. Trevor sat at his wife's bedside, wiping her face with a damp cloth.

"She's too weak to wash herself. Don't tire her."

"I'll just be a few moments. Will you feed the dogs? I didn't have time yet."

"Sure."

Carmel lips twisted into a weak smile. "He loves animals more than people. I think that's why he's a vet."

"A veterinarian? I didn't know that."

"Yes."

"I brought you a cookie," Anne said, "and a bottle of juice."

Carmel twisted her head away to face the wall and shuddered. "I'm not hungry."

How could she get through to this woman? "You are getting weaker. Did you walk by yourself to the bathroom this morning?"

Carmel turned to the wall. Her narrow scapulas tented her pyjama top, two sharp-peaked mountains of ivory silk. Anne felt a rush of compassion for her, so ill and yet still caring about what she wore to bed.

She put her arm around Carmen and helped her to sit. The bones of the young woman's shoulders could be an anatomy lesson for beginners. "A small bite and sip of juice."

Carmel sighed and took the cookie. She nibbled an edge and then drank from the straw Anne held for her.

"Good," Anne said.

Trevor opened the door and the dogs bounded in. Carmel smiled and reached down to pat their heads. She loves animals too,

Anne thought. Perhaps she could use that to reach the starving girl.

Outside the room she hurried down the hall to Thomas.

Anne opened the door to their room to find Thomas sitting by the fire, his dark head bent over a book. He preferred to read in print on paper, not on an electronic device. She lugged hers everywhere. With the power out, she was left with nothing to read when it lost its charge. He raised his head and grinned, his eyes crinkling, and a look of triumph on his face.

"What's happened?" she said.

"We got through to Culver's police."

"Culver's? How on earth did you do that?"

"The old man who owned this place had call letters for Vermont. One of them was in Culver's and it still worked. They're calling Bancroft OPP for us."

She sat on the arm of his chair for a moment and he pulled her onto his lap and kissed her. She rearranged herself and snuggled into his arms. "That's good news. In the meantime, we should talk about who and how?"

"You don't want to wait for the cops?"

"I don't think we can afford to. I think the motive is Hamish and his trust fund."

She moved to the chair across from his. Thomas raised his eyebrows and sat back. "To control the baby is to control the money?"

"David changed his will today, but the courts are unpredictable and there have been two murders in this family. I think we should make a list of who has drugs and who had opportunity."

Anne, restless when she was thinking, prowled the room, stopping to check the storm—still snowing—before coming back to the fire. She shivered and drew a soft cashmere blanket around her shoulders.

"Who heads the list?" Thomas said.

"Brad and Andrea, one or both. She has a pharmacopeia of drugs and several that would do the job."

"What about opportunity?"

"I'm trying to remember that dinner before Vanessa died. If she was poisoned, and I think she was, someone must have slipped drugs into her wine or her coffee."

"Do you remember who filled her glass or brought her coffee?"

Anne took paper from the desk between the windows, dropped back into her chair, and propped a book on her knee. She listed the names of all the others, starting with Brad and Andrea. A second column she devoted to known access to drugs. "Several people, including me."

"What about motive for killing Vanessa?"

"With her out of the way, are the courts less likely to favour David, a single man, over say the grandmother and uncle or the aunt and her husband? I'm going to make a chart."

"Brad, Andrea, Eloise, Trevor, and Carmel all had access to narcotics."

"How do you figure Trevor and Carmel?"

"He's a vet. If he has his bag, he'll have something with him to tranquillize an animal. Powerful sedation."

"And Eloise?"

"Tylenol threes for migraine."

"What about Mike?"

She looked at him and shook her head. "I have no idea. You've been working with him. Do you think he's a killer."

"I don't think so."

"Beth and Kevin?"

"Normalcy personified. I haven't heard anything about them wanting kids, or needing money, or hating Vanessa, or anything like that."

"Who hated Vanessa?"

"Brad, Andrea, Eloise."

"Who had opportunity to poison David?"

"Again, me. I made the coffee and brought it in. Trevor handed it around, and someone else brought out the cognac. I forget who."

"Likely Brad."

She nodded her head. Brad was always bringing drinks to people, especially Andrea. "Possibly. I don't think Eloise would poison him and I don't think she had opportunity anyway."

Anne drew another column, and headed it *motive.*

"Where are we?" Thomas said.

"Motive. Hamish for Brad, Andrea, Trevor and Carmel. Hatred for Vanessa or wanting David for Eloise. Nil known for Mike, Beth or Kevin."

"So nothing definitive?"

"I think we can eliminate Eloise, and I don't see what Mike had to gain."

"True and he's been helping to get to the police."

Anne leaned back in her chair and sighed. "I hope they get here soon."

"When the weather breaks. I have to go back down. We're running out of wood."

"I'll be down to see about food, more food."

Outside Anne and Thomas's room, the killer turned the doorknob and edged it ajar. He listened. That woman was getting too close and she was a doctor. People told her things, thinking it was safe. It wasn't. She'd have to go. Lots of doctors committed suicide. She'd have to.

He returned to his room and his stash of narcotics. She was a small woman; it wouldn't take much to sedate her and then he would take her into the bush.

Chapter Twenty-Eight

Thomas dropped his pile of split wood on the floor and shucked off his parka. He was stacking the logs in a basket by the wood stove when the door to the kitchen from the stairs opened, and Kevin bounded in.

"Hi, I wondered if you needed any help?"

"Sure. Can you stack in the porch while I finish these?"

Afterwards, they sat at the table over cups of coffee.

"How's the investigation going?" Kevin asked.

That's a first for him, Thomas thought. Hadn't been interested before.

"Not so well. It's hard to narrow down the list."

"Motive?"

"Almost everyone."

"We don't. I want to get my wife out of here and away from her crazy family."

"Brad or Andrea?"

"Both. That stunt she pulled and his getting her booze whenever she wants it. And now she's sick, maybe dying, and Beth is full of guilt, even though her mother never loved her."

That was odd. Why tell him that? They weren't buddies.

"What's the problem with the mother?"

"Beth won't have kids and won't try to adopt Hamish. Andrea seems to think that any connection with Karen will be good enough for the courts."

"You don't want kids?"

"Not right now."

What did that mean? They couldn't or wouldn't?

"Anne's worried about Andrea."

"Yeah. She shouldn't have come here. None of us should have, especially Trevor and Carmel. That poor woman has been sick for years."

"You know them well?"

"Not so well, but everyone who's ever been around them knows that."

"You live in New York City?"

"Yeah, and that's something else that gets up Andrea's nose. She thinks we should work in Toronto."

"So you're closer to her? Most mothers would want that, wouldn't they."

"The only reason she wants us there is so we are in the correct jurisdiction to adopt Hamish."

"She sounds obsessed."

Kevin raised a single eyebrow at him and snorted. "What gave you that idea? The plunge into the ice storm with the baby? She's a drunk and a fool. I'm going to keep Beth away from her."

"Big trust fund."

Kevin reared back and anger flashed across his face. "What's that supposed to mean? We don't need a baby's money. We manage on our incomes fine. I'm not saying we'll stay in the US forever, but for now, it suits us and a baby isn't in our plans."

So much for that, Thomas thought. If he was telling the truth.

"You didn't say if you made any progress with the radio?" Kevin said.

"Yeah, we reached the OPP. They're coming when it clears."

"Did you tell them about the downed wire."

"Yes."

"Good. Shouldn't be long now, then?"

"No."

Relief flooded Kevin's face. He wasn't very old, Thomas thought. Maybe 30 or so. They had time for kids and other plans. "Can't be too soon for me. Let me know if you need any help later."

"I'll do that."

Kevin clambered up the back stairs, passing David on his way into the kitchen.

David swung into a seat at the table, poured a cup from the carafe and cocked his head towards the stairs. "What was that about?"

"He wanted to know the state of the investigation. Apparently, Andrea and Beth don't get along because Andrea wants her to try to adopt Hamish and they don't want kids, at least not now."

David shook his head and his lips drew into a long hard line. Besieged, angry, and fed up, Thomas thought. A lot of jolts this weekend.

"That woman will try anything to get Hamish."

"And Brad to get the money? Including murder?"

David drew his brows together and frowned. "I wouldn't go that far, but when this is over, they're not getting access if I can stop it."

Better change the subject, Thomas thought. He was getting agitated and there was work to be done. "We're almost out of wood in the shed. What say we try to find some deadfall in the forest?"

David pushed away from the table and stood up. "Sure."

They suited up in snowmobile gear and took snowshoes from the hooks by the mudroom door. Before they left, Anne came into the kitchen, tense lines around her eyes betraying her worry. Again, too much on her, Thomas thought.

"Are you looking for Mike?" Anne asked.

Thomas shook his head. "No, we're going to look for deadfall. The wood supply is almost out and we need that before we can worry about where he might have gone or why," said Thomas.

"What about Mike?" said David.

"Took off. Remember last time, he arrived suddenly. Maybe it's his way?"

"To leave without saying anything? I doubt that. He usually tells me when he's going and why would he go anyway? He knows it's not safe in the bush," said David.

"We'll look for signs," Thomas said and followed David out the door.

Their snowshoes carried them over the fresh snow to the forest beyond.

"We want old trees, not growing ones brought down by the storm," said Thomas.

They entered a fantasy landscape, a foreign planet of misshapen trees humbled by ice that transformed them into statues of monks, clothed in green and white. Silence. No birds, no forest creatures startled into flight. And then an explosion of sound as a forest giant fell, toppled by its burden.

"It will take a while for the forest to recover," said Thomas.

"The bush has been through worse. A fire gutted this area in the last century and logging took the old growth before that. It will survive."

"I hope we will too."

"They know we're here now."

"The killer knows they're coming, so whatever the long game, it's got to happen soon."

"You think there's a plan."

"Sure."

Hillocks of snow defined locations where dead trees might be found, but too often all they found was a boulder or bush. But they worked steadily for an hour, releasing deadfall from the ice, and piling it on the sled.

On the way back, Thomas spotted a dark shape on the ground, a few yards distant from the path they were following. "You see that," he said.

"Where?"

"There to the left," he said, pointing.

David veered off the path and bounded over to the spot. "Get over here, Tom. It's Mike."

David knelt beside the body and felt for a pulse. Nothing. Blood, lightly covered with snow, stained the area around the body pink. "He's been here a while."

"No hope," said Thomas, squatting beside David.

"None."

"Why kill Mike?"

"Why kill anyone. Is the radio working?"

"At times. We'll leave him here but we better blaze the trail on the way back."

David axed a raw wound in the tree that guarded the body and they hauled the wood and their heavy news back to the lodge.

The kitchen, warm from the stove and fragrant with the aroma of baking bread, welcomed David and Thomas when they came through the back door.

Anne chopped vegetables at the sink, piling the results on a platter beside her. "You found more wood. Terrific," she said.

"That's not all we found. You better sit down."

Thomas's dark eyes, full of worry, met hers. What could have gone wrong, she wondered. What have they found? She dried her hands and folded them on the table.

Thomas and David took chairs opposite. "Mike has been killed," Thomas said.

Anne fell back in her chair. A wave of cold washed over her and she shuddered. An accident. Surely it was an accident. "No. Oh, no. Did he touch a live wire out there or did a tree fall on him?"

"No. It wasn't an accident."

She gripped her hands together until the knuckles turned white. She tried to ask the next question but her throat closed and she struggled for breath.

Thomas swung around the table and put his arms around her. "Don't struggle. Take a shallow breath," he said, as she had taught him to say when the panic hit her.

In a moment she had control. She reached up a hand to pat his. "Thank you. How did he die?"

"Stabbed, likely. We didn't disturb the body but there was blood, a lot of it, on the snow and under the most recent fall."

"He died where you found him?"

Tears stung her eyes and she covered them with her hands. She had liked Mike, liked his casual approach to life.

"Yes."

"Sedated and taken there or overwhelmed by someone bigger and stronger."

"No one here is like that. He must have been sedated. A woman couldn't have shifted him."

"No."

"That only leaves three."

"Should we tell the others?" asked David.

"No, I don't think so. That would put you at risk, too," said Anne. "Can you get a message out, Thomas?"

"Maybe."

"Can you hide it?"

"Hide what?"

"The radio, before it's destroyed."

Eloise sat by Hamish's bedside, listening to his calm breathing. He was definitely better, she thought. She'd ask Anne about cutting back on his puffers today. Although she had dosed him every hour, now she was giving him Ventolin every three hours. Multi-coloured children's clothing filled laundry baskets around her. Soon the children would run out of clean clothes. She hadn't packed enough for a long stay. Across the room, Olivia chose a bright red crayon.

"What are you drawing today, Olivia," Eloise said.

"A man."

"What man?"

"A tall man."

Eloise chuckled. All men were tall to Olivia. She dug through the pockets of the children's clothes. From Hamish's toddler jeans, she fished out two Lego people and a tiny grey stone flecked with gold. In another pocket, she found a brass button. Now matter how hard she tried to keep things away from him that he might choke on, he still picked up stray objects. Olivia was different. Her pockets contained treasures she confiscated from some of the rooms she was allowed in, and some she wasn't. Her blue terrycloth housecoat gave up a stray lipstick(hers) and a sample bottle of scent. She unscrewed the cap. Vanessa's. Had she been in there again? No, the door was locked.

Deeper in the pocket, she found a paper folded small. She smoothed it out on her knee.

A marriage certificate. The simple document recorded the marriage of Vanessa Donlands and Mike Lawrence, ten years before. A prior marriage. Had they been divorced then? She must show this to Anne and Thomas. They could decide if David should know.

"Olivia, viens ci."

Olivia scampered over to Eloise and stood in the circle of her arm.

"Where did you find this paper?"

Olivia hung her head. "Spanking."

"You know it was Vanessa's and she's gone so you won't get into any trouble if you tell me the truth. And no spanking, I promise."

"It was in her box with all the pretty jewellery, underneath."

"Why did you take it?"

"Someone was coming."

"Where did you go?"

"Into the closet."

"Did Vanessa find you?"

"No. When the man left, she went to sleep, and I ran out of the room. She was covered with red paint, and I was scared she will blame me."

"Would blame you. It's okay, but I want you to tell Anne. Can you do that?"

"Oh, yes. I like her."

"You go see if she is in the kitchen and say I want to see her. Okay?"

Olivia raced from the playroom and down the stairs.

Somewhere a door closed with a faint click.

After Anne left, Carmel slept. Later, Trevor opened the drapes and called to Carmel. "It's time to wake up, Carmel."

No response.

He hurried to her bedside. Her eyes, sunken in her pallid face and surround by skin so dark it almost looked bruised, fluttered towards him and away.

"Can you talk, sweetheart?"

A moan was her only answer.

"Should I call Anne?"

"No, I hate her. She won't help me. She makes me eat."

"You have to. They won't let you have a baby if you don't."

"Where were you?"

Her querulous voice accused him and tears rolled down her cheeks. He sat on the bed next to her and brushed the tears away. "Right here with you, sweetheart."

"But I woke up and you weren't here."

"You were dreaming, I think."

"Yes, dreaming."

Carmel drifted off the sleep, Trevor sat back in the chair and watched her breathe. Soon he would have her out of here, they would sue for Hamish, and she would get better.

Olivia scampered down the stairs to the kitchen, but Anne wasn't there. A plate with chocolate-chip cookies sat on the counter. Anne would let her. She grabbed a cookie, stuffed it into her pocket and ran up stairs and along to Anne's room. She listened. Adults were talking. She wasn't supposed to interrupt but Eloise sent her. It would be okay. She knocked.

"Come in."

Anne and Thomas sat close together on the couch, like Vanessa and David did. Maybe they would try to get married too. She could ask— No, she wasn't supposed to ask people questions about themselves either. Too many things she wasn't supposed to do. Sometimes she forgot.

"Olivia. What is it? Come sit with us."

Anne held her arms out and Olivia climbed onto her lap.

"Why have you come to visit us?" Thomas asked.

Olivia snuggled into Anne's soft chest. "Eloise said I should come."

"Why, dolly?" asked Anne.

"Because I drew a picture and she wants you to see."

"Okay. I'll come."

"And I'll work on the radio," said Thomas.

Chapter Twenty-Nine

fter Olivia left, Eloise settled back to mend one of Olivia's jeans. She started at a knock at the door to the nursery. Her heart pounded, and her voice trembled when she called out, "Who is it?"

"David.

Her heart gave its little jump, as it always did when he opened the door. Should she tell him? It had only been a few days since Vanessa died, but it felt as though a long year had passed.

David reached into the crib and stroked Hamish's unruly hair. The child stirred but slept on, his slow, soft breathing free of wheeze."How is he?"

"Much better. I think he will be able to get up this afternoon. He wants to escape the crib."

Eloise brushed a hand across her face and turned to the window. A stray beam of sunshine, filtered through the pines, scattered itself across the snow like diamonds and crystals.

"The rest of us want to leave the house, but he'd be happy to play on the floor, poor guy."

"Yes," she said. "Hamish loves to play with his Lego and his trains."

His eyes caught hers and something, something different passed between them. Eloise caught her breath before she spoke. "David, I—"

"Eloise—"

"You first," he said.

"I'm sorry about Vanessa."

Was that what she meant to say? No. She wanted to tell him she loved him and that Vanessa didn't and never would. But she never would say that to him, never.

"Tragically, she died, but I think I was going to make a terrible mistake."

A mistake. What did David mean, mistake?

"Oui?"

"Oui. I don't think I knew her. So much I overlooked. Her attitude towards the children. Her dislike of the simple life we lead here. The way she was with the dogs. And every time we disagreed, she sulked and withdrew her...affection until I apologized, even if she were at fault. And all that time, I missed seeing the person I was falling in love with."

"And who?"

His eyes, full of pain and longing, kept their lock on hers. "You must know. "

"I only know how I feel. I love the children, and I loved you from the moment we met."

He reached for her, but she turned away. "What if they say I killed her because I was jealous? I hated her for how she treated the children and for how she treated you."

"You didn't kill her, and neither did I. Anne and Thomas will find out who did. What's important is that we love each other."

She walked into his arms, and as they closed around her, she was home.

Anne and Olivia met David in the hall on their way to the nursery.

"We're going to Eloise," said Olivia.

"Eloise has something to show me," said Anne.

"Any idea what? She didn't mention anything when I was there."

"Something Olivia drew, perhaps?"

"A new drawing? I'll come back and see it later, shall I?"

Olivia bounced up and down. "Yes, yes. Come now."

She took David's hand and pulled him towards the nursery door.

"Not now. I need to talk to Thomas. I'll be back later."

Olivia stuck out her lip for a moment but then trotted down the hall, and Anne followed her inside the room. Eloise rocked Hamish on her knee, caressing the strawberry-blond hair that fell in tendrils across his forehead.

"Does he have a fever?"

"Non, non."

Anne listened to his chest but heard nothing alarming. She sat opposite Eloise, noting her flushed face and bright eyes. "Are you ill," Anne said.

"No, no. I'm so happy. David—"

"Yes."

"He—"

"Yes."

"He says I don't have to go and—"

"It's the *and* that has you glowing, I imagine. You had something to show me."

"Yes. Olivia, bring Anne what you found."

Olivia hung her head and drew circles with her toe on the carpet. "She'll be mad."

"No, she won't."

"I won't be angry with you, Olivia," Anne said.

Olivia raced to the dresser and carried the paper, grubby from its stay in Olivia's pocket, over to Anne.

What was this? A small oblong of paper, the shape of a receipt, similar the one in her safety deposit box at home, proof of her marriage to Michael, lay in her hand. "She was married to Mike?"

"So it would seem."

"What sort of scam was she running and was Mike part of it? Were they planning to blackmail David?"

"No, no. He hasn't said anything about that. Nothing like that. You can't think David killed them."

"Others might, Eloise."

Eloise's elegant fingers wiped tears from her eyes. "Find out who is doing this. It's not David. It's not."

Olivia patted Eloise's shoulder and glared at Anne, her lower jaw thrust forward. What a striking resemblance to Cooper, Anne thought. A little fighter.

"I will. Olivia, did you draw something today?"

The little girl handed the picture to Anne.

A body, outlined in black, its middle covered with red crayon, lay on a bed, one arm dangling over the side.

"Who is this, Olivia?"

"Vanessa."

"When did you see her?"

Olivia hung her head. "I'll get in trouble."

"No, you won't. Were you in Vanessa's closet? Did you lose your little pony?"

"Yes. Vanessa might spank me."

Anne put her arms around Olivia. "No one will spank you now. What happened when you sneaked out of the closet?"

"She was sleeping, and her dress was all covered with red paint, and she would say I did it. I opened the door and ran into the hall. A man was at the end of the hall."

"Did he see you?"

"No."

"Do you know who it was?"

"I don't remember."

"Maybe, you will. Draw some more pictures today."

"I will."

She turned to Eloise. "Don't let her talk about this. We have to keep her out of danger."

Eloise paled and her face crumpled. "He, whoever it was,

wouldn't kill a child."

"He might. Keep Olivia with you. I'm going to talk to Thomas."

Downstairs, Thomas fiddled with the dials of the battered old radio in the front window. The speakers crackled with static as he sought a voice or the chattering of a telegraph key. When David spoke behind him, he startled and swung the dial.

"Sorry, Tom. I hope you weren't closing in on something."

"No. I'm trying to reach the OPP in Bancroft. I found their call letters and channel but so far, nothing."

"Depends on the atmosphere?"

"Yes, somewhat. At least I don't have to worry about enemy agents standing outside my door, waiting to burst in."

"What are you talking about? What enemy agents?"

Thomas twirled around in his chair, and David pulled one up.

"In WW11, thousands of radio-equipped agents communicated with the allies from inside occupied Europe. They worked in the cities and the country, in networks or alone. The guys alone in the cities had no one to watch for the scanning vehicles in the streets nor had any way except their own tradecraft to prevent discovery. Their work was vital, but the Nazis captured many of them because they got sloppy, talked to a girlfriend, or broadcast from the same location at the same time instead of randomly. The solo ones in the country were dependent on the goodwill of the communities and their own skill. Some were embedded with the Underground. It was the amateur radio operators who alerted the people of France that the invasion was coming on June 6, 1944. The radio service in London broadcast a nineteenth-century poem by Verlain on June 1."

He quoted the poem,

"Les sanglots longs

Des violons

De l'automne.

The verse signalled the resistance to be ready for further alerts, and that Operation Overlord would begin within two weeks. "

He continued, " On June 5, at 23:15 hours they broadcast the next three lines, a signal for the resistance to begin sabotage on the railway system.

Blessent mon coeur

D'une langueur

Monotone.

The invasion began before dawn on the 6th, a few hours later."

"How do you know all this? Was ham radio a hobby when you were a kid?"

"No," said Thomas. "I had some training in it for a job I did."

The radio spoke behind him, asking for him to respond to the call letters for the OPP. But moments later, the signal disappeared.

Beth sat by the dying embers of the fire, reading by the light of an oil lamp. The light from both flickered across the pages. In some ways, she enjoyed the solitude, the break from the frantic pace of their life in New York, the race to get to work, to shop, and to socialize. Her work for the city engrossed her, but recently she had trouble with a new boss who was empire-building, she thought, and saw her as a rival.

Kevin loved his job, but between them, they made barely enough. He wanted to move out of the city, to somewhere they could have more room and perhaps even buy. But the commute? How awful it would be.

Her mother wanted them to move to Toronto, and they could or at least, Kevin could. How hard would it be for her to get another job there? Not much scope for historians. Perhaps she could write? She wanted to expand her thesis into a book. Their condo in New York, though tiny, would sell for enough for them to buy something decent in Toronto, or maybe a suburban city.

Kevin opened the door and sat opposite her.

"Has something happened?"

"I had a conversation with Thomas. He was probing for a motive."

"For you or us?"

Appalled, she reached a hand out to him across the narrow space that separated them.

"Does your mother or Brad know that we are up against it financially?"

"I don't think so. I didn't say anything."

"But you haven't talked about vacations or new clothes? Maybe she got the idea?"

"She would make it up as she went along, anyway."

"I can't imagine that they would think we would try to adopt Hamish and Olivia to solve a financial issue. All we have to do is move out of New York."

"While I sat here, I enjoyed the solitude and peace. I thought when we came that I would be stir-crazy in a day, but even with all the trouble, I love it here."

"So do I."

She crossed to him and snuggled on his lap. "Would you move back to Canada if we could get jobs?"

"That's a thought. Let's talk about it when we're home and back in our normal life."

"If we ever are. What if Mom or Brad—"

"You can't think that."

"She's obsessed, and he's broke."

"A reason to adopt, to go to court, not to kill. No, Beth."

She lay her head on his shoulder, he stroked her hair, and she relaxed into his arms. Safe with him, she thought. Always safe. "Did you find out when we might get out of here?"

"They got the radio working and contacted someone in Thomas's home town. They're calling the OPP."

"So, soon?"

"Let's hope so."

"I'm going down to help Anne in the kitchen."

"I'll walk with you."

Chapter Thirty

Anne ran down the front stairs to the living room. The evening sun slanted through the bay window at one end, lighting up Thomas's dark hair and casting a shadow behind him across the Navaho carpet on the floor.

David sat beside him, intent on Thomas's hand swinging the dial slowly to catch a voice or the tap of a telegraph key. Neither heard Anne as she walked across to them. Both whirled around when she spoke.

Startled, she stepped back. "Thomas, we have to talk. David, I think Eloise wants you in the nursery. Olivia is upset."

David sprang from his chair and strode across to the stairs.

"What's going on?" said Thomas.

"Olivia was a witness to Vanessa's murder."

Thomas frowned and his face echoed the worry she felt. "How is she a witness? Where was she?"

"In the closet in Vanessa's room. She doesn't know what she saw. She drew a picture of the body but thought the blood was red paint and she would be blamed, so she said nothing. I haven't talked to her too much. I'm so afraid she's in danger now, too."

"Would she say if she recognized David's voice?"

"You think—"

"No, but we have to consider it."

"Eloise found a marriage certificate in Olivia's pocket."

"Whose?"

"Vanessa and Mike's."

"What kind of scam were they running? And did David know?"

Anne shook her head. She was sure David wasn't a killer, nor Eloise. But the motives were stacking up. "I don't think so. I wondered what Mike would do with the knowledge."

"Like?"

Anne paced to the window and watched the wisps of sunshine being swallowed by dark clouds. Not more snow. "Blackmail comes to mind."

"Not a motive to kill Vanessa unless you think there are two killers here."

Two killers. No.

"No, I don't.

"So that leaves Trevor or Brad or Kevin."

"Motive for Kevin?"

"None that I know. Not Hamish, anyway. They can have their own kids, and I don't think they need the money. Not enough to kill for."

"The other two have the same motive—custody of Hamish—for Vanessa's death and the attempt on David and if Mike was trying blackmail, the same motive to kill him."

"Means?"

"Both."

Behind them, the radio crackled and a voice, so clear it sounded as the speaker was beside them, asked for VA3eew to respond.

"VA3eew, over," said Thomas.

Anne's hands gripped his shoulders.

"Who is this? Over."

"Thomas Beauchamp. I'm here at a lodge owned by David McKnight. We've had two homicides and one attempt here and need your assistance. Over."

"We'll come as soon as we can put a helicopter in the air. Depends on the weather. Is there a landing site? Over."

"To the west of the building. We also have two very ill women, one of them is elderly with pneumonia and the other with severe anorexia nervosa and will need medivac for them. Over."

"As soon as we can. Over and out."

"No timeline," said Anne.

"The weather's improving. The OPP may arrive here later this evening."

"Dark clouds outside. Maybe snow."

"I'll try for a weather report."

Thomas's worried eyes looked up into hers.

"I'm going to cook."

"Just you?"

"Eloise has to guard Olivia, and she can't leave Hamish. I can ask Beth to help me."

"Be careful."

"I will."

Back in the kitchen, Anne fished in her purse for her miniature Swiss army knife and dropped it in her pocket. Too small to be much good, but she felt better with it there.

Beth opened the door to the kitchen. What a domestic scene, she thought. Wearing a red apron that announced St. Émilion in a lovely script, Anne relaxed at the scrubbed pine table, pouring from a fat-bellied, brown teapot. A Brown Betty. Beth hadn't seen one in years, not since she left home to go to university.

"Can I help you in any way," she said to Anne.

"Thank you. I'm going to have a quick tea before I start. Would you like a cup?"

Beth sat down opposite her. Anne's hand shook slightly when she poured the tea. Not so relaxed, Beth thought. Worry lines around Anne's eyes and dark circles under them reflected the stress she must be under. Perhaps she knew more than she and Kevin did? Of course, she did, and she saw the bodies. Even a doctor would be affected by that. "Are you okay?" she said.

"Tired. It seems as though we've been stranded here forever."

"Yes. But you've been terrific what with making the food for everyone and taking care of the sick. Thank you for helping my mother."

Anne smiled at her, a smile that reached the green eyes and smoothed out some of the worries. "My job, after all."

"We didn't do anything to anyone."

Why had she blurted that out? What would Anne think now?

"I don't think you did. You're under strain, too. Is it your mother?"

Beth covered her face with her hands and sobbed. "And my brother. Mom's crazy focus on Hamish and now she's dying. She focussed on Brad the way she concentrates on Hamish."

"Why?"

"We lost our dad and she was so in love with him. Now it's Brad and Hamish."

"Perhaps this brush with death, arising out of her obsession, will get through to her."

"I think it's too late."

Anne reached across the table and took the younger woman's hand. "It's never too late while she lives."

They sat in silence for a few minutes and then Anne said, "We'd better get on with it. Better they're all fed."

"Tell me what to do."

Their final meal, Anne hoped, as she stood at the window, looking out across the field. Water dripped from the roof, overflowing the eves. The trees in the distance still wore their caps of white, but the weather gauge read two degrees celsius, high enough to melt the snow and ice, but not before morning. That wouldn't solve the problem of the downed trees across the roads, the electrical poles snapped in two, and the crumpled transmission towers. Snow fell, tidying the landscape, renewing the clean blanket overlying everything. No helicopter tonight, she thought.

Chilli for dinner, the lodge cook's standby. She had stored five containers of the stuff in the freezer and plenty of rolls. She would never eat chilli again, Anne thought.

Beth set the table and took butter from the fridge. "I think we should keep this in the porch. The fridge is too warm now."

Eloise brought the children down and seated them at the table. Hamish, his breathing regular, perched in his high chair and banged his fists on the tray.

"Are you hungry, Hamish?" Anne asked.

"Yes, he is," said Olivia.

"Remember to let Hamish use his words," Eloise said.

"Older sister syndrome," said Anne.

"Yes. Olivia's so quick she answers before he understands the question."

Olivia squirmed in her chair and reached for a roll.

"Not yet, Olivia. We must wait for the others."

"Let them go ahead. We rang the bell some time ago, but only you have come," Anne said.

"I'll go for Kevin," Beth said. "He'll be deep in a book."

The door to the stairs crashed open in advance of Brad stumbling through, his face contorted with fury. "You. Why aren't you with my mother?"

"Aren't you with her?"

"I'm not a nurse."

"Neither am I. I have other patients and it appears I'm the cook as well. Or did you come down to make dinner for us all?"

"Make dinner? All you did was thaw something the cook made."

"You're welcome to the job."

Anne tossed the oven mitts to him and headed for the door to the living room.

"Wait, wait. I'm sorry. I'm worried about Mom. I think she's having more trouble breathing, and her colour is worse."

"Did you give her another puffer?"

"I think it's empty."

"You can use Hamish's. He doesn't need it anymore," Eloise said.

"I'll come up in a few minutes," said Anne. "In the meantime, grab a bite to eat and take some of this broth up to your mother."

Brad swallowed great spoonfuls of the savoury stew, crouched over his bowl like a dog protecting his dinner. A few moments later, he left with a mug of broth and a roll.

Eloise followed."I'll take him the puffer. The mask would be too small for Andrea."

After she left, Anne sat with the children. Olivia loved chilli and emptied one bowl and started on another. Hamish played with a roll, tearing it into tiny pieces. Anne guided his spoon to his mouth. She listened for Eloise's footsteps on the stairs. Was it safe to let her go alone with Brad? She wiped Hamish's face and then opened the door to the stairs. Eloise, surprise on her face, met her.

"You're all right," Anne said.

"You were worried about Brad? I gave his mother two puffs and told him to give her two more in an hour. Was that right?"

"Yes. I'll look in on her before that."

"Her colour was bad but she was a little better after the puffer."

"Eat some food while you have time."

Thomas swung through the door to the living room with Trevor at his heels. "The OPP think they can get a helicopter in the air when the snow lets up. Not before morning, though."

"OPP? What about air ambulance? What about my wife? Why are you here, wasting time on food when she's dying."

He raced around the table and towered over Anne. Thomas moved in behind him.

"Food is what she and everyone else needs, Trevor. I'll come up to her when I finish here," said Anne.

"And what about those kids? Are you leaving them with a murderer?

David, silent in the doorway during Trevor's rant, said, "The children are protected."

"Are they protected from you? We can look after them, Carmel and I."

"Carmel can't look after herself."

"She could if she had a chance, if she were his mother."

"Not a chance. And remember if I'm dead, Anne and Thomas are the guardians, at least until Eloise and I marry."

"What? David, you—"

"We'll talk later, Eloise. Leave, Trevor."

Facing Thomas and David, Trevor backed away and scuttled up the stairs.

"He has an angry voice, again," said Olivia.

"When did you hear his angry voice before," asked Anne, sitting beside the little girl.

"When he was cross with Vanessa. Only he whispered."

"Did you see him in Vanessa's room?"

"No. But I saw the man in the hallway when I ran out. I drew him."

"When? I didn't see that picture, Olivia," said Eloise.

"I was bad."

"Because you were in Vanessa's room. So you hid the picture?"

"Yes."

"What should we do?" said David.

"Guard the children until the cops arrive."

"I'm going to see Carmel."

"I'll come with you," said Thomas.

"Take him out of the room while I try to get her to eat. If he lets me."

Beth and Kevin came in as they went out and sat with Eloise and the children. Behind her, Anne heard Olivia's delighted laugh. Kevin was good with kids. It was a shame they didn't want or couldn't have their own. Which was it, she wondered?

※

Back upstairs in the nursery, Eloise tucked the children into bed and sat in a rocking chair across from David, her eyes scanning his face.

"What did—"

"I wanted—"

"You first," said Eloise.

"I'm sorry I blurted that out in front of everyone."

He held his breath, or so it seemed to her. On the mantel, a round-face alarm clock ticked quietly to itself. The comforting squeak of the rocking chair kept time with it. Her restless hands rubbed the smooth arms of her chair, the ancient pine polished by who knew how many other mothers.

"I love you, Eloise. I want you to marry me."

What should she say? She loved him so much, but did he love her for herself or for her as a mother to the children.

"Too soon. Perhaps we should wait to talk about this when our lives are back to normal."

His whole face collapsed, his eyes downcast, the corners of his mouth dragged down too. He looked so unhappy Eloise longed to go to him and promise him anything.

"Do you love me? You said you did."

"Yes, from the first moment. But four days ago, you were going to marry Vanessa. I, we, need time to be sure."

"But you won't go away?"

"No, no. I want to care for the children if you want me to."

"Of course."

"Will you be my mommy?" asked a tiny voice from the bed in the corner.

"Perhaps. You go to sleep, and we'll talk about it when we go home."

"When will we go home, Daddy?"

David's voice caught as he answered her. She had never called him anything but Uncle David.

"Tomorrow. We'll go home tomorrow."

They sat in opposite chairs, in the light of the fire that faded as the flames burned down, their eyes on each other and on the children. David added a white birch log that flared and crackled. He caressed her head as he passed, and she caught his hand for a brief moment.

Tomorrow.

Left alone with Thomas, Anne finished washing out the bowls while he dried. After, she placed a cup of broth and two crackers on a sandwich plate, one of glass set, decorated with multi-coloured mobiles, that she'd found in the cupboard.

"I'm coming with you," said Thomas.

"Yes," said Anne.

She wasn't sure that Trevor was the killer but she knew she didn't want to be alone with all that rage. Upstairs, she knocked on the door and went in, Thomas at her heels.

"Why is he here?"

"To watch you."

"I—"

"Don't try. Go sit over there while I talk to Carmel."

Trevor, sullen and resentful, his pale skin flushed with rage or shame, hovered in a corner, guarded by Thomas while Anne examined Carmel.

"How long has she been unresponsive?" she said.

"What?"

"How long since she talked to you?"

"Earlier today. She said she didn't want to see you."

"I can't rouse her. Come over here and call to her."

Trevor knelt by the bedside and took Carmel's hand, calling her name over and over, louder and louder.

"She won't answer," he said, his words swallowed by his sobs.

"She's in a coma now."

"I'll try again on the radio," said Thomas.

"Isn't there anything you can do?"

His pale blue eyes pleaded with her, but she couldn't help, not there.

"Nothing. Carmel needs a hospital and intravenous. You stay with her. I'm going with Thomas."

"No, stay."

"There's nothing I can do for her."

Anger flashed across his face, replaced in an instant with a polite mask.

"Thank you for helping her."

Anne looked back at the door, but he was bent over Carmel, calling her name.

Chapter Thirty-One

Back in the living room, Anne snuggled into a leather armchair. Thomas wrapped a wool Hudson's Bay blanket around her shoulders. He sat at the desk in the window and edged the dial forward on the radio, found Channel 53 and broadcast his call letters. "This is VA3eew, calling OPP Bancroft. Please respond. Over."

Nothing. Thomas tried again on another channel. "This is VA3eew, calling OPP Bancroft. Please respond. Over."

The radio crackled, and a professional voice responded. "We hear you VA3eew. Give us an update, please. Over."

"One woman in a coma, one deteriorating rapidly. Running out of food. Two children here and two corpses. Can you send assistance? Over."

"A medivac helicopter will be in the air at first light. One of ours crashed but another will be here in the morning and will reach you. Over."

"Your pilot? Did he survive? Over."

"She. Yes, she did. Do you need to talk to a doctor here? Over."

"No. One of us is a doctor. Over and out."

Thomas swivelled to Anne, who sat nearby. "He said a medivac at first light. They lost a helicopter in the storm, but the pilot survived."

"This awful weather."

"I'm going to try to reach Culver's Mills again. I'd like someone to check the house and the housekeeper. They may have had this storm too."

"I'm going to finish up in the kitchen and leave it in some kind of order for when the staff gets back."

"You don't have—"

"I know. I'll just do a little."

"I don't like you alone out there."

"I'm a few feet away. It will be fine."

Trevor sat beside Carmel. So still. When did he last hear her voice? When did he last see her smile? What if she died. He sobbed against her cold hand. It was all that woman's fault. She took away her hope. She wouldn't promise to speak for them, to let them adopt Hamish. The boy belonged with them. He was his sister's child. Maybe if he talked to Anne again, she would agree.

"I'll find her, my love, and force her to help us."

Thomas knocked at the door of the nursery and walked in. Eloise held Hamish and Olivia cuddled on David's lap. A lovely family, Thomas thought. He hoped they'd make it.

"I wanted to tell you that a medivac helicopter would be here in the morning. I'm trying to call someone at my company to notify my pilot to come up."

"We don't have to go out in the first bunch now that the children are well," said David.

"I can try that now."

"No, I want to stay until everyone has gone."

"The children and I will stay with David. It would be too upsetting for them if we went and left him behind."

"That's fine. I'm going to notify Brad and Andrea."

He walked the few steps to Andrea's room and knocked, waiting for an answer before he opened the door.

"Yes?"

"Thomas. Can I come in?"

He went through the story with Brad, assuring him that his mother would go out first.

"Can I fly with her?"

"Likely not, if they have to take both women. But—"

"I can't let her go by herself."

"I'll call my pilot to pick you up at the same time.

"What about you and Anne?"

"We'll wait for his next trip."

Across the hall, there was no answer from Trevor. Thomas looked inside. Carmel lay still and pale, her breathing so slow he had to wait to be sure she was alive. Anne better look at her again. And he'd left her in the kitchen, alone. Why did he do that? He raced down the stairs to find her.

Chapter Thirty-Two

Trevor burst in the door to the kitchen where Anne stood at the sink, the last of the dishes in her hand. "You. You made her worse."

Anne whirled, her heart racing, afraid of the rage and insanity she heard in the high voice. The glass she held slipped from her fingers and shattered on the pine floor. "What are you talking about, Trevor? How did I make her worse?"

She took a broom and dustpan from the closet and swept.

"Leave that alone. You know how. You took away her hope, our hope. You said she needed to eat or she wouldn't be allowed to adopt."

"The dogs will come in, and the glass will cut their feet. First, that is true and second, I hoped to convince her to eat and drink a little. She's dying, Trevor. She was dying when you brought her here instead of to a hospital. Why did you do that?"

"Stop that and listen to me. I don't care about the damn glass. And now you won't stay with her, you bitch. Call yourself a doctor. All you want to do is play house with Thomas. You don't care."

His eyes, wild with fury, bored into her. She edged towards the door to the stairs, the broom held in front of her like a sword. If she could reach it, open it, and scream, Thomas would come. But Trevor saw her move and, crashing chairs from out of his way, wrenched the broom from her grasp, and grabbed her arms. She fought back, kicking and punching, aiming for his genitals as she had been taught, but he was a big man, towering over her. He put one arm around her, swung her around, and covered her mouth with the other. He dragged her through the door to the mudroom, banging her hip against the frame. Fiery pain shot down her leg. She clawed at the arm holding her.

Trevor grabbed duct tape from the shelf, used his teeth to cut a strip, and plastered that across her mouth. Now with a hand free, he half-carried, half-dragged her out the door and onto the ice and snow.

Maybe someone would see. Thomas would come looking for her. She had to slow him down. He held her under one of his arms as he struggled with her through the deep snow, breaking through the ice below at every step. Once he fell, and she managed to reach the little knife in her pocket and pry it open. The blade sliced her thumb and blood dripped down her arm and into her sleeve.

Where was he taking her? The forest beyond the clearing grew closer. Would they find her? Or at least her body before the bears or the coyotes. She shook blood on the snow to leave a trail.

Upstairs, Olivia is standing at the window. "When can I go outside to play."

"When the ice melts, you can go out. First, we're going to fly to Toronto, to our house. You can play outside there."

"Can we take the dogs to the park?"

"Yes."

Olivia jumped up and down at the window, hitting the glass with her hand. "Eloise. Eloise. The man with the red hair is hurting Anne."

Olivia screamed and hit the glass harder.

"Olivia, stop that," said Eloise, coming over to the child.

"He fell down and he made Anne fall too. Eloise, Daddy, look. Look."

Her daddy looked and ran for the door. He was shouting for Thomas.

"Eloise, what is the man doing to Anne? I'm scared."

She wrapped her arms around Eloise and cried.

Thomas raced down the stairs. The kitchen stood empty; winter blasted in from the outside door. Where was she? Behind him, the staircase door opened again.

David hurtled into the room and grabbed Thomas's arm. "Trevor has her. Across the field towards Mike's body."

Thomas shrugged him off and ran for the door. He didn't wait for boots but followed footprints across the field, oblivious to the snow and ice filling his shoes. Behind him, he heard the door slam.

Half-way across, signs of a fall; blood stained the snow. Anne's or Trevor's? Ahead the two figures struggled, but then they disappeared into the trees. He raced forward.

Beside him now, David gasped, "Careful. Who knows if he has a gun?"

They moved silently under the pines. Ahead something fell , and birds flew up, angry and afraid.

Chapter Thirty-Three

Birds flew up out of the bushes as he pulled her through, one bird so close its wings brushed her hair. Vicious buckthorns raked her face, and she closed her eyes to protect them. She hoped there was no poison ivy, but it didn't matter. What did anything matter? She only had moments to live. Her hand gripped the knife, leaving only the little blade. She would stab him if she had a chance, but where? His groin. If she could reach the artery, or even give him enough pain so he would let her go.

He stopped, and she stumbled out of his grasp, looked down and tried to scream. Mike's dead eyes stared up at her.

"Lie down."

She shook her head at him. He came closer to grab her arms. Before he did, she raised the hand with the knife and stabbed his neck.

He roared and backhanded her across her mouth. She fell and thrust upwards, blindly, hoping to reach his groin. He bellowed and tried to kick her but fell, blood spurting from his neck. His carotid. She hit his carotid. She crawled away from him as he reached for her. She couldn't save him.

He whispered. One word. What was it? Can? No, Carmel. The light faded from his eyes, and he toppled on top of her. A dead weight. If she couldn't get him off, perhaps she would be gone too. So heavy. She shoved, but he didn't budge. She fell back into the snow and yanked the tape from her mouth. In the distance, she heard shouting. Thomas. Was that Thomas? He would find her. She closed her eyes.

Chapter Thirty-Four

Anne lay motionless on the blood-stained snow. Trevor straddled her body, his head forward over hers, one hand gripping a knife. Fear squeezed Thomas's heart. She couldn't be dead. He couldn't lose her when they were so close.

He bellowed, racing towards Anne, "Trevor. Get the hell off her."

He grabbed the hand that held the knife.

David stood on the other side of Anne. "I think he's dead, Tom. How—"

Anne's voice came in a hoarse gasp. "Thomas, I knew you would come."

"Thank God."

He knelt beside her and brushed snow off her face. She opened her eyes and managed a smile, sort-of a smile. Trevor's weight on her chest crushed her. She tried to talk, a strangled gasp. She tried again. "Pull him off of me. I can't breathe."

David and Thomas rolled the body and helped Anne to her feet. She held a tiny knife in her right hand. Was that all she had? A penknife?

"Give me the knife."

She dropped it into his hand and shuddered. "Again, Thomas. Again."

He held her against him while she sobbed.

"I thought I'd lost you."

His lips brushed her hair.

"Tom, I'm going back to tell the others," David said.

"Don't tell Carmel," Anne said. "If she's awake, don't tell her yet."

"Did you check Trevor?" Thomas said.

"Yeah. She stabbed him in the neck and maybe the groin. Most of the blood's from his neck."

Anne turned from Thomas and vomited, staining the snow behind her with yellow bile. Thomas grabbed her arms and stared into her face, willing her to listen to him.

"You had to do it. He'd already killed two people."

She took so long to recover from Spain and now this.

"Take me back, Thomas. I'm so cold."

Together they retraced the footprints to the house. Partway, Thomas pointed to the bloody trail.

"Whose blood?"

"Mine. I cut my thumb when I opened the knife."

Brave, he thought. She's so brave. He held her closer as they stumbled together towards the lodge.

In the nursery, Eloise hugged Olivia to her as they waited for someone to come out of the bush. Olivia turned frantic eyes to her. "Why was the man with the red hair taking Anne away? He's a bad man. He hurt Vanessa."

"Yes, he's a bad man."

"Look, look. Daddy's coming. Daddy's coming."

David strode across the field and behind him, Anne and Thomas. Anne was walking. Thomas was holding her, but she was walking.

"Anne is okay. Anne is okay."

Olivia jumped up and down and rapped with a little fist on the window. Below, David looked up and smiled and waved.

"Can we go downstairs? Can we?"

"We must wait for Daddy to come up. He'll come soon."

A few moments later, David opened the door and stared for a moment. Why was he staring? Olivia stood beside her, holding her hand. Hamish, lay in the crib, his bottom in the air as always when he slept. And then she knew. He was looking at his family. She held out one arm and gathered him in. He lifted Olivia and clung to them.

"It's over," he said. "It's finally over."

"Trevor?"

"Yes."

"Is the bad man coming back, Daddy?"

"No, baby. No."

He kissed the little girl's forehead and hugged them both closer.

In the kitchen, Anne collapsed onto a press-backed kitchen chair and drew a deep breath. The knobs of the carving drilled into her back, and she shuddered.

Thomas wrapped an Afghan throw around her shoulders and threw another log into the stove. "Tea?"

"Yes, tea. Thank you."

Thomas poured hot water from the reservoir in the stove into the kettle and set in on a heated burner. In a few moments, it boiled, and he made a potent brew. When it was ready, he poured two cups, loaded both with sugar and milk and set one in front of Anne. "Lots of sugar, as I know you order for shock."

"Yes, good idea."

How strange she felt. Numb and detached. She killed Trevor. He would have killed her. She remembered the rage in his eyes and shivered.

"Are you cold? I'll find another—"

"No. I remembered the way he looked. So angry. So angry. He said I took away their hope and drove him to do this."

Thomas took her right hand and held tight. "They had no hope, and he killed Vanessa in cold blood. You were a threat, getting too close."

"But his fury?"

"Perhaps he needed it to murder an alert woman rather than a comatose one."

"Comatose. We have to check Carmel."

She half-rose from her chair, but Thomas shook his head. "Later. You have to recover first."

"She might be dead."

"There's nothing you can do if she is."

So pragmatic. She used to think she was pragmatic, but lately she was a confused mass of emotions.

He gripped her hands, covering both of hers with his. "I thought I lost you."

She smiled, tried to smile. "I knew you would come."

"Always."

Yes, always. When they left this awful place, they would talk about always.

"I'm ready to tell Brad and Andrea," she said.

"Let's go up."

Chapter Thirty-Five

Anne stood beside him when Thomas knocked on the door and opened it at Brad's muttered come in.

"What do you want?"

"Let me look at Andrea first," Anne said. "Have you noticed any change?"

"I think she might be breathing a bit easier."

Anne checked Andrea's colour and listened to her chest. "How do you feel?" she asked.

"Better."

Her breathing was less laboured, and the rales in her chest were clearing. She might make it.

"Yes. Your chest sounds better too. Did you eat or drink this morning?"

"I brought her some tea and toast. Where were you all?"

Thomas spoke from across the room. "Chasing Trevor. He abducted Anne and dragged her to the forest to kill her."

Andrea gasped, and the blue tinge to her lips deepened. Anne held the puffer below her nose and gave her one dose, and another.

"Beth?" she gasped.

"We haven't told her."

"He didn't hurt her?"

"I'll go see Beth," said Thomas and hurried from the room.

"Trevor is the killer?" said Brad.

"Yes. Was. He's dead."

"What kind of place—"

"It's not the fault of the lodge but this conflict over Hamish. He thought if they had Hamish, Carmel would recover. And then there's the money."

"He killed two people? Two people."

"And tried to kill two more. And there were others on Trevor's list, Brad. Andrea, you. Eloise."

"He was insane."

"Yes. Perverted love for Carmel."

"How is she?"

"Comatose, last I saw her. When Thomas comes back, we'll go there."

"Helicopters will be here in the morning. One for Carmel and Andrea and one for you and the others if they want to go."

"What about you?"

"Later."

Thomas knocked on the door of Beth and Kevin's room, and walked in at Kevin's shouted invitation.

Beth and Kevin sat near their fireplace, wrapped in sweaters, enveloped in blankets from the bed. "Thomas. What brings you here? Do you have news?"

"Yes. Rescue is on the way for Andrea and Carmen. The police are coming—"

Kevin leaned forward towards Thomas, his face contorted with worry. "What will you tell them?"

"I have more bad news. Beth, it was Trevor who has been killing. He killed Vanessa and Mike and tried to kill David and Anne."

"Anne. Is she—"

"Fine. She fought back, and Trevor is dead."

Colour left Beth's face, and she trembled. "But why?"

"We think he was focussed on getting Hamish for Carmel and eliminating everyone who stood between them and the baby."

She stood up and took a step towards the door. "My mother?"

Kevin leaped up and took her arm.

"She's fine. Anne is with her. You know her first thought was of you and you of her."

"It was?"

"I have to go—"

"We have to go," Kevin said.

Anne and Thomas found Carmel deep in a coma, unresponsive to her name, although she moved and brushed away her hand when Anne applied pain.

"She may survive. How many more hours until morning?"

"Ten or thereabouts."

"Should we call the OPP again?"

"Yes."

Thomas built a fire, and they sat for a while in front of the leaping flames.

"The radio?"

"I'll try again. Sometimes it's easier to get through at night."

Anne listened while he called the letters of the OPP and his explanation of what had happened when he reached them.

"They'll be here in the morning," he said.

"Can you sleep? Should we go up?"

"Yes."

✳

Kevin knocked at the door to Andrea's room.

"Who is it?"

"Kevin and Beth."

"Come in."

Kevin pushed open the door, walked with her over to the bed where her brother sat, clutching Andrea's hand. Brad's eyes, red-rimmed and swollen, focussed on their mother.

"Mom," she said, her voice low and gentle.

"She can't hear you, Beth. Speak a little louder," Brad said.

She stood beside him. Andrea opened her eyes, looked past them at something just beyond, but turned them on her children. "Beth."

"I'm here, Mom."

Her face crumpled, and the blue of her lips darkened. "I'm sorry—"

"Don't worry; don't worry. We'll talk when you're better."

"Not getting—"

"Yes, you are. Yes, you are. You can't leave us."

Brad heard the pleading in his sister's voice, remembering when their father had left. *Don't leave us*, she cried after him as he stormed out the door, and she turned on their mother in a rage, blaming her for their father leaving. A few months later he was dead, alone on the side of a northern road. It had all gone to hell then.

Beth's hand crept into his, he hesitated, and squeezed her fingers, holding them gently, lest, bird-like, they flutter away.

The memory of a smile drifted across Andrea's face, and she closed her eyes again.

"They're coming," Beth said, half a question, half a hope.

"Yes. Thomas reached them, and the helicopter will be here as soon as the weather breaks."

"You go if you can. We'll come as soon as possible."

"Yes. We'll talk about what to do."

Her eyes met his and tears crept down her face. He hadn't seen her cry since their dad left.

"She'll be all right. She'll be in a hospital soon."

She nodded her head and leaned against Kevin, but she didn't let go of Brad's hand. A ray of late afternoon sunshine crept through the crack in the drapes and played for a moment across Andrea's face.

Chapter Thirty-Six

Anne stood at the kitchen window, watching the shadows lift. The morning brought blue skies and sunshine. The ice shrouding the fir trees glowed an unearthly green, like a rock formation on Venus. Glints like flashing diamonds danced across the snow. Above the trees, a helicopter roared its approach.

Behind her, Thomas, David, Eloise and the children waited.

"They've come," she said.

Beth and Kevin clattered down the stairs. "Which one?" said Beth.

"Orange. The medical one."

"Thank God. They'll take Mom now, won't they?"

"Yes."

Another engine announced the arrival of a white and orange Ontario Hydro truck in the lane. Men in winter overalls, orange to match the vehicles, carrying chainsaws, waved but didn't come across the wire.

Thomas and David strode across the field to meet the paramedics. Once the crew came inside, Anne took them upstairs to Carmel. They stabilized her with an intravenous and took her downstairs and went back for Andrea. Once both were ready and they had spoken to base, they flew off.

Brad watched from the window. "When will the next one be here?"

"The police should be next," Thomas said.

"But it's all over. We can tell them who the killer was and that he's dead."

"We'll see."

Would they charge her, Anne wondered. Or would they look at the size of Trevor and the size of her, at the bruises rapidly developing on her arms and across her face and conclude the story was true? After her experience in Bermuda, when she was accused of murder and in Spain, when a policeman made a false case against her, she had less trust.

A helicopter on approach roared over the house and settled in the spot flattened by the medivac. Uniformed men dropped to the ground and headed her way.

Hours later, after interviews that stretched into the night, the police left, taking Brad with them to his mother at the Bancroft Hospital. The detectives accepted the story of the events that had occurred. Eloise told them about watching Trevor drag Anne across the field and showed them the documents Olivia had taken from Vanessa's room. Anne recounted the attempt on David's life and what she did to defend herself.

"You'll hear from the Crown Attorney or us," the lead detective said. "We think you should go to the hospital and have those bruises documented."

"We'll go to Peterborough in the morning."

"Let us know."

"Yes."

David and Eloise, Anne and Thomas waved to Brad and the departing police and sat in the kitchen. David got a bottle of cognac from the living room and poured.

Anne swallowed and shuddered as the fiery liquid hit her

damaged throat. "When..." she croaked. She tried again. "When will you go back to Toronto?"

"I'll go back after the police cleanup crew has been here. It should only take a day or two."

"And you, Eloise. Will you and the children stay?"

"Not for too long. We have to call the staff back and arrange for food and so on. They will come later today. And you?"

"Our helicopter will be here about 10:00 am, tomorrow or rather later today."

Anne reached for Thomas's hand. Soon, she thought. Soon they would be out of this nightmare of a place and home.

Chapter 37

L ater that day, as the helicopter roared and rose towards the sky, Anne said, "Will you ask the pilot to circle the lodge, Thomas? I want to wave goodbye to the children and Eloise said she would bring them outside."

Thomas spoke to the pilot through his headset and the craft tilted into a turn. Below, the red roofs of the McKnight home formed a cross against the pristine snow. Two adults, one with a yellow snowsuited burden, and a child trudged towards the dock. At the sound of the helicopter, they looked up and waved.

Olivia, in a neon-green snowsuit, jumped up and down, waving wildly and then fell, her arms swirling to make a snow angel. Eloise and David holding Hamish, made thumbs-up towards them and Eloise threw them a kiss with her white-mittened hand.

"They're going to be happy, I think," said Thomas.

"Yes and successful parents if the courts allow the adoption."

"I'm sure they will. Are you writing a letter to the court?"

"Yes, as soon as we're home. We have to talk."

"Here?"

"The only times we're not involved with a host of others and several corpses is when we're in a plane. Can the pilot—"

"Andrew, turn off communication for a few minutes," he said.

"Yes, sir."

"Now he can't. What—"

"Yes."

"Yes, what."

"Yes to you, to our life together, to moving forward together. If you still want that?"

"How can you ask?"

He drew her into his arms and kissed her. From inside his parka, he drew out a battered jeweller's box in royal blue leather. "This was my grandmother's," he said. "I've been carrying this around for three months. I hope it fits you now or we could have it resized."

Anne opened the box on an exquisite emerald, surrounded by diamonds, set in antique gold filigree. "It's so lovely."

Thomas slipped the ring on her finger. She stretched her hand and smiled up at him as the sun caught the diamonds and reflected a rainbow of colour onto the grey bulkhead.

"Perfect," he said. "Where would you like to honeymoon?"

She snuggled led into his arms. "Somewhere we won't find any bodies."

He laughed and said, "Agreed."

About the Author

Virginia Winters is the author of Dangerous Journeys, a series of suspense novels with a genealogical theme. The Ice Storm Murders is the 6th. She also wrote Painting of Sorrow, the first in the Deadly Art Series.

Virginia lives in Lindsay, a small Ontario town, with husband George and standard poodle Cully.

Also by Virginia Winters

Dangerous Journeys

Murderous Roots

The Facepainter Murders

No Motive for Murder

The Child on the Terrace

The Jewelled Egg Murders

Deadly Arts Mysteries

Painting of Sorrow

Short Story Collection

A Superior Crime and other stories

Boxed Sets

Dangerous Journeys Books 1-4